Serving Trouble

Serving Trouble

A Second Shot Novel

SARA JANE STONE

AVONIMPULSE

An Imprint of HarperCollinsPublishers

Running Wild copyright © 2016 by Sara Jane Stone.
An Excerpt from *Hard Ever After* copyright © 2016 by Laura Kaye.
An Excerpt from *Wild at Heart* copyright © 2016 by Tina Kline-smith.
An Excerpt from *The Bride Wore Starlight* © 2016 by Lizbeth Selvig.

EPub Edition MARCH 2016 ISBN: 9780062423849
Print ISBN: 9780062423856

10 9 8 7 6 5 4 3 2 1

For every woman who has ever wondered
if she was strong enough.

Acknowledgments

JOSIE FAIRMORE WALKED into my imagination four year ago and never left. I owe Amanda Bergeron a huge thank you for helping me craft Josie's story. And to everyone at Avon Impulse—thank you for everything you do, from the covers to the marketing to the publicity!

A heartfelt thank you to Jill Marsal for reading dozens of early drafts of this story and for finding a home for the Second Shot series!

I also must thank my husband for always being my hero when I need one. When we left the hospital with our son still in the neonatal intensive care unit . . . I would have crumbled without you by my side. I never thought I would be strong enough to face that again. And yet, nineteen months later, when we found ourselves in the NICU again, you were right there by my side.

I owe a debt of gratitude to the doctors and nurses who cared for my babies. Thank you for helping them through those first few days and weeks. I can't imagine my life without my kids—even when they refuse to go to bed the night before a big deadline.

To all of my readers, thank you for embracing the cast of characters in the Independence Fall series. And thanks for asking for more of Noah and, of course, Josh!

Chapter One

"I DROVE TO the wrong bar."

Josie Fairmore stared up at the unlit sign towering above the nearly vacant parking lot, her cell phone pressed to her ear. Nothing changed in Forever, Oregon. Everything from the people to the names of the bars remained the same. The triplets, who had to be over a hundred now, still owned The Three Sisters Café downtown. Every car and truck she'd sped past had the high school football team's flag mounted on the roof or featured on the bumper. And her father was still the chief of police.

Nothing changed. That was why she'd left for college and never looked back.

Until now.

She'd blown past the Forever town line ten minutes ago. She'd driven straight to the place that promised a rescue from her current hell. And she'd parked under the sign, which appeared determined to prove her wrong.

"Josephine Fairmore, it is ten thirty in the morning," Daphne said through the phone, her tone oddly stern for the owner of a strip club situated outside the town limits. "The fact that you're at a bar might be your first mistake."

Damn. If the owner of The Lost Kitten was her voice of reason, Josie was screwed.

"When did they take the 'country' out of Big Buck's Country Bar?" Josie stared at the letters above the entrance to the town's oldest bar. She twirled the key to her red Mini, which looked out of place beside the lone monster truck in the lot. She should probably take the car back to the city. The Mini didn't belong in the land of four-wheelers, pickups, and logging trucks. The red car would miss the parking garage.

But I can't afford the parking garage anymore. I can't even pay my rent. Or my bills. . .

"Big Buck gave in three years ago," Daphne explained, drawing Josie's attention back to the bar parking lot. "He decided to take Noah's advice and get rid of the mechanical bull. He wanted to attract the college crowd."

"He got rid of the bull before I went to college." And before his son left to join the United States Marine Corps. She should know. She'd ridden the bull at his going away party.

With Noah.

And then she'd ridden Noah.

"Well, Buck made a few more changes," Daphne said. "He added a new sound system and—"

"He changed the name. I guess that explains why Noah came home." She glanced at the dark, quiet bar. The hours posted by the door read "Open from noon until the cows come home (or 3am, whichever comes first!)."

"He served for five years and did two tours in Afghanistan. Stop by The Three Sisters and you'll get an earful about his heroics," Daphne said. "But from what I've heard, Noah didn't want to sign up for another five. Not after his grandmother died last year."

"You've seen him?" Josie looked down at her cowboy boots. She hadn't worn them since that night in Noah's barn. She'd thought they'd help her land the job at the "country" bar. But now she wished she'd worn her Converse, maybe a pair of heels.

"Yes."

"At The Lost Kitten?" Why, after all this time, after she never responded to his apologetic letter, would she care if Noah spent his free time watching women strip off their clothes? One wild, stupid, naked night cut short by her big brother didn't offer a reason for jealousy.

But the fact that I told him I love him? That might.

"No. I bumped into him at the café." Daphne hesitated. "He didn't smile. Not once."

"PTSD?" she asked quietly. She couldn't imagine walking into a war zone and leaving without long-lasting trauma. The things he probably saw . . .

"Maybe," Daphne said. "But he's not jumpy. He just seems pissed off at the world. Elvira was behind the counter that day. She tried to thank him for serving our country after he ordered a burger. He set a ten on the counter and walked out before his food arrived."

"He left his manners in the Middle East." Josie stared

at the door to Big Buck's. "Might hurt my chances for getting a job."

"I think your lack of waitressing or bartending experience will be the nail in the coffin. But if Noah turns you down, you can work here."

"I'd rather keep my shirt on while I work," Josie said dryly.

And he won't turn me down. He promised to help me.

But that was before he turned into a surly former marine.

"You'd make more without it," Daphne said. "Or you can tell the hospital, the collection agency—whoever's coming after you—the truth. You're broke."

"I did. They gave me a payment plan and I need to stick to it." She headed for the door. "I ignored those bills for months. Besides, what kind of mother doesn't pay her child's medical bills?"

The kind who buried her son twenty-seven days after he was born.

Daphne didn't say the words, but Josie knew she was thinking them. Her best friend was the only person in Forever who knew the truth about why she was desperate for a paycheck. If only Daphne had inherited a restaurant or a bookstore—a place with fully clothed employees.

"He has to agree," Josie added. "I need that money."

"I know." Daphne sighed. "And I need to get to work. I have a staff of topless waitresses and dancers who depend on me for their paycheck. Good luck, Josie."

"Thanks." She ended the call and slipped her phone

into the bag slung over her shoulder alongside her wallet and resume.

She drew a deep breath. But a churning feeling started in her belly, foreboding, threatening. She knew this feeling and she didn't like it. Something bad always followed.

Her boyfriend headed for the door convinced he was too young for a baby . . . Her water broke too early . . .

She tried the door. Locked, dammit.

Ignoring the warning bells in her head telling her to run to her best friend's club and offer to serve a topless breakfast, she raised her hand and knocked.

"Hang on a sec," a deep voice called from the other side. She remembered that sound and could hear the echo of his words from five long years ago, before he'd joined the marines and before she'd gone to college hoping for a brighter future—and found more heartache.

Call, email, or send a letter. Hell, send a carrier pigeon. I don't care how you get in touch, or where I am. If you need me, I'll find a way to help.

He'd meant every word. But people changed. They hardened. They took hits and got back up, leaving their heart beaten and wrecked on the ground.

She glanced down as if the bloody pieces of her broken heart would appear at her feet. Nope. Nothing but cement and her boots. She'd left her heart behind in Portland, dead and buried, thank you very much.

The door opened. She looked up and . . .

Oh my . . . Wow . . .

She'd gained five pounds—well, more than that, but

she'd lost the rest. She'd cried for weeks, tears running down her cheeks while she slept, and flooding her eyes when she woke. And it had aged her. There were lines on her face that made her look a lot older than twenty-three.

But Noah . . .

He'd gained five pounds of pure muscle. His tight black T-shirt clung to his biceps. Dark green cargo pants hung low on his hips. And his face . . .

On the drive, she'd tried to trick herself into believing he was just a friend she'd slept with one wild night. She'd made a fool of herself, losing her heart to him then.

Never again.

She'd made a promise to her broken, battered heart and she planned to keep it. She would not fall for Noah this time.

But oh, the temptation . . .

His short blond hair still looked as if he'd just run his hands through it. Stubble, the same color as his hair, covered his jaw. He'd forgotten to shave, or just didn't give a damn. But his familiar blue eyes left her ready to pass out at his feet from lack of oxygen.

He stared at her, wariness radiating from those blue depths. Five years ago, he'd smiled at her and it had touched his eyes. Not now.

"Josie?" His brow knitted as if he'd had to search his memory for her name. His grip tightened on the door. Was he debating whether to slam it in her face and pretend his mind had been playing tricks on him?

"Hi, Noah." She placed her right boot in the doorway, determined to follow him inside if he tried to shut her out.

"You're back," he said as if putting together the pieces of a puzzle. But still no hint of the warm, welcoming smile he'd worn with an easy-going grace five years ago.

"I guess you didn't get the carrier pigeon," she said, forcing a smile. *Please let him remember.* "But I need your help."

NOAH STARED AT the dark-haired beauty. Her white T-shirt hugged her curves, and her cutoff jean shorts sent him on a trip down memory lane. And those boots . . .

The memory of Josephine Fairmore had followed him to hell and back. He'd tried to escape the feel of her full lips, the taste of her mouth, her body pressed up against his . . . and he'd failed. He'd carried every detail of that night in the barn with him to basic training. Right down to her cowgirl boots. He'd dreamed about Josie in a bikini, Josie on the mechanical bull, Josie damn near *anywhere*, while hiking through the Afghan desert. He'd spent years lying in makeshift barracks wanting and wishing for a chance to talk to her while staring into her large green eyes.

And yeah, who was he kidding? His gaze would head south and he'd let himself drink in the sight of her breasts.

He closed his eyes. He'd spent two long deployments hoping for an email, a letter—something from her. He'd wanted confirmation that she was all right. But she never wrote. Not once. She'd reduced him to begging for tidbits from Dominic. Not that her brother had volunteered much more than a *She's fine. Stay the hell away from her.*

But she wasn't fine.

He opened his eyes.

"You needed help and you sent a pigeon?" He released his grip on the door and rested his forearm against it. "You could have called."

"I thought it would be better to apply for a job in person," she said, her voice low and so damn sultry that his dick was on the verge of responding.

Not going to happen.

There were a helluva lot of things beyond his control. His dad's health. His grandmother's heart failure while he was stationed in Bumblefuck, Afghanistan, fighting two enemies—and one of them should have been on his side. And the fact that the only time he felt calm, in control, and something bordering on happiness, was at the damn shooting range.

Still, he could control his own dick.

But why the hell should I?

He let his gaze drift to her chest, down her hips, and down her slim legs. He'd wanted her for five long years and here she was on his doorstep. What was stopping him from pulling her close and starting where they'd left off five years ago? He wasn't the good guy worried about her big brother's reactions or her reputation. Not anymore. Nothing he'd done in the past five years had left him feeling heroic. So why start now?

She crossed her arms in front of her chest. And while

he appreciated the way her breasts lifted, he raised his gaze to meet hers.

"I'm not hiring," he lied. Big Buck's needed a waitress or two, another bartender, and a dishwasher to keep up with the crowds pouring in from the nearby university, desperate to bump and grind to house music. But if she worked here, well hell, then he'd have another reason he shouldn't touch her. He had a rule about messing around with his female employees. It was bad business. He'd worked too hard to turn Big Buck's into something to fool around with a waitress or a bartender.

She raised an eyebrow and nodded to the Help Wanted sign he'd put up in the window. "Someone put that up without asking you?"

Shit.

"I recently filled the position," he said, searching for an excuse that didn't touch on the truth.

"I'm too late." She shook her head. "Perfect. I guess I should have gotten up the nerve to come home a few days ago."

He glanced over her shoulder and saw a red Mini parked beside his truck. It looked like a toy next to his F-250. And apart from the driver's side, every cubic inch appeared stuffed with bags.

"I thought you liked Portland. Greg from the station said you haven't been back here in a few years," he said, knowing he should close the door and end the conversation. If he let her in, if he handed her an application followed by a Big Buck's apron, he couldn't touch her. That wasn't much different from the past five years, or the ones before the going away party, but she hadn't spent the past decade or so within arm's reach.

"It didn't work out," she said.

"They don't have jobs up there for someone with a fancy degree? I bet you could do a lot better than serving drinks."

She blinked and for a second he thought she might turn around and walk away, abandoning her plea for help. "I took a break from school, lost my scholarship, and then dropped out," she said.

"What?" He stared at her. "Dominic never said—"

"My dad didn't know I'd quit school until recently. And I don't think he told Dom," she said quickly. "My brother has enough to worry about over there. Like not getting killed or . . ."

"Worse," he supplied. Like losing a limb or a fellow soldier. Yeah, Noah knew plenty of guys who'd lost both. But he'd worried about losing respect for the band of brothers serving with him because they'd flat out refused to treat the woman busting her ass alongside them with an ounce of decency . . .

Except Dominic would probably have stepped in and saved the woman before she was attacked. Josie's brother wouldn't let the situation get beyond his control and then try to pick up the pieces.

"There are worse things than dying out there," he added, trying to focus on the here and now, not the past he couldn't change.

"Yes."

He kept his gaze locked on her face as he stepped back and placed his hand on the door again. He was ready and willing to slam it closed. She could tempt and tease him, but he refused to take his eyes off her face. Hell, he knew better than to play chicken with her breasts. Right now, with the way he wanted her, he'd lose that game.

First, he needed some time to process. He wanted space to think about the fact that things hadn't worked out for her in Portland. He needed her to leave before he pulled her close, wrapped his arms around her, and offered comfort. Before he begged to know every damn detail about what had happened.

No, he needed her gone. Because he'd learned one big life lesson from his time with the marines: he wasn't a hero. He couldn't let old habits take over, pushing him to save her. He wanted Josie's hands on him, her lips pressed against him . . . not her problems dumped at his feet. And if Josie was back in the town that had insisted on labeling her wild, holding her solely accountable for losing her panties in a hay wagon ride, then something had gone horribly wrong in Portland.

"I'm sorry," he said. "I can't—"

"I need a job, Noah." She wasn't begging, merely stating a fact. But desperation and determination clung to her words. Never a good combination.

Noah sighed. "Do you have any waitressing or bartending experience?"

"Not exactly." She forced a smile as she uncrossed her arms and riffled through the worn black leather shoulder bag. She withdrew a manila folder and handed it to him. "But I brought my resume."

Propping the door open with his foot, he took the folder and opened it. He read over the resume and tried to figure out how a series of babysitting gigs related to serving the twenty-one-and-older crowd.

"You took a year off between working for these two families." He glanced up. "To focus on school?"

"No." Her smile faded. "I can serve drinks, Noah. I'm smart and I'm good with people. Especially strangers. And now that you've taken the "country" out of Big Buck's, I'm guessing the locals don't camp out at the bar anymore."

"Some still do." And they gave him hell for telling his dad to remove the mechanical bull. Five years and the people born and bred in this town still missed the machine that had put the "country" in Big Buck's Country Bar. Some dropped by to visit the damn thing in his dad's barn. But he'd bet no one had ridden it like Josie in the last five years.

He closed the folder and held it out to her. "Why are you so desperate to serve drinks?"

"I owe a lot of money."

Another fact. But this one led to a bucket of questions. "Your father won't help you?"

She shook her head. "This is my responsibility. He's giving me a place to stay until I get back on my feet."

The don't-mess-with-me veneer he wore like body armor cracked. If someone had hurt Josie . . . No, she wasn't his responsibility. Whatever trouble she'd found—credit card debt, bad loans—it wasn't his mess to clean up. He'd spent most of his life playing superhero, first on the football field, later for his family, and then for his fellow marines. But his last deployment—and the fallout—had made it pretty damn clear that he wasn't cut out for the role.

He couldn't help Josie Fairmore. Not this time. And he sure as hell couldn't give her a job that would keep her underfoot. He couldn't pay her to work for him and want her at the same time. It wasn't right. Maybe he was a failed hero. But he still knew right from wrong.

"Look, I need experienced waitresses and bartenders." He stepped away, ready to head back to the peace and quiet of his empty bar.

"So you haven't filled the positions?" she asked.

"I—"

"Please think about it." She removed her foot, offering him the space to slam the door. "If you can't help me, I'll have to take Daphne up on her offer to serve topless drinks at The Lost Kitten. And I'd rather keep my shirt on while I work. But one way or another, I'm going to pay back what I owe."

She turned and headed for the red Mini. He stared at her back and pictured her bending over tables. One look at her bare chest and the guys at The Lost Kitten would forget what they planned to order. He hated that mental image, but jealousy didn't dominate his senses right now.

He'd witnessed a woman sacrifice her pride and her dignity for her job. He'd fought like hell for her and he'd failed her. He couldn't change the past. What happened to Caroline was out of his hands now. Even if he wanted to help, he couldn't. She'd disappeared. If and when Caroline resurfaced, she'd be the one charged with a crime. Unauthorized absence. And his testimony? The things he'd witnessed? It wouldn't matter.

But Josie was standing in his freaking parking lot.

"I'll give you one shot," he called. She stopped and turned to face him. Her full lips formed a smile and her eyes shone with triumph.

"A trial shift," he added. "If you can keep up with a Thursday-night crowd, I'll consider giving you a job."

"Thank you," she said.

"Come back around four. And don't get too excited. Your babysitting experience won't help with a room full of college kids counting down the days until spring break."

He closed the door and turned to face the dark interior of his father's bar. Giving her a shot didn't make him a hero. But it would give him a chance to figure out why she needed the money.

Chapter Two

BY FIVE O'CLOCK, Josie had learned one valuable lesson in cocktail waitressing—wear cowboy boots, sneakers, or flats. Even flip-flops would have been better than the two-inch black high-heeled strappy sandals she'd selected for her first shift. The shoes matched her fitted black shift dress. The low-cut neckline was designed to entice without screaming, *Hooters, here I come!*

But her feet ached.

Noah—the man she'd dreamed about throughout her teenage years, transitioning those innocent what-if-he-asks-me-out scenarios to X-rated daydreams after their ride on his mechanical bull five years ago—moved behind the bar, pouring beers and mixing drinks.

She headed to the waitress station and keyed in an order. Thank goodness Big Buck had upgraded to computers when they took out the bull. She hit enter, heard the ticket print behind the bar, and turned to scan the room.

College students milled about the space, filling the booths and high-top tables. But the dance floor with its large stacks of speakers remained empty. Noah had told her the music would start at 9pm. A Seattle DJ was spinning tonight and another bartender would arrive then too.

She glanced at her future boss—well, he would be if she passed the trial without kicking off her heels and running around barefoot taking orders—and caught him grinning from ear to ear. "There's your smile," she murmured.

Noah twisted the top off a beer bottle with his bare hands. He held the drink out to a man with movie star looks wearing a Moore Timber T-shirt.

"Planning to visit the range anytime soon?" Noah asked, only he wasn't talking to the man who oozed charm as if it were a habit he couldn't quite break. Noah had turned to the woman with the cover-girl-ready face and long blond hair on the stool beside him.

"I'm always game," the man jumped in. "But I'm not ready to move beyond the viewing area."

"Safest place for you and the dog," Noah said with a laugh. He'd picked up the drink ticket and was mixing the college students' fancy cocktails while he spoke. "Where is Hero tonight?"

"In the truck for now," the woman said, her smile fading. "When it picks up a bit, I might bring him in if that's OK with you. I have his service dog vest."

"Hero's welcome here, Lena. Anytime." Noah offered a soft smile. "If you're planning on sticking around, you'll want to get him soon."

"Thanks." Lena looked relieved. "Josh is meeting us here after work. He ended things with Megan."

Josie studied the woman's model-like features and tried to remember if they'd met five years ago when she'd lived in the Willamette Valley. She came up blank. But the charming man, flashing Lena a grin designed to lead to the bedroom—she knew him. He was older than her for sure. But that smile . . .

"My brother claims he wants to settle down," the familiar man added. "And Megan made it clear she wasn't interested in long-term. Beats me why she stuck around this long if she wasn't."

"Chad," the picture-perfect Lena, who needed a service dog in crowded bars, said.

She was still a mystery, but hearing that name, Josie remembered.

Chad Summers.

Half her high school class had had a crush on him. She knew girls who'd driven over to Independence Falls just to watch him play pickup baseball games in a field. She'd been too busy mooning over Noah. And later, Travis Taylor, the boy she'd mistakenly believed could fill the good-guy-football-hero void in her life. Except Travis failed the good-guy test when he'd unleashed his temper on her instead of saving it for the field.

"First step to keeping your job," Noah said, walking over to the service end of the bar and setting down the filled drinks. His smile had vanished. "Stop drooling over the customers."

"I wasn't . . . I recognize him," she protested.

"Chad's engaged now. Or will be soon," Noah continued. "To Lena. Don't even think about messing with her. I've seen her shoot."

"You're still visiting the gun club?"

He nodded grimly. "Every chance I get."

He hadn't lost his smile. But doom and gloom seemed to be his default in her company. Maybe if she made him laugh—

"To Noah," a man who looked a decade or two older than her father called out. "For his service."

Four men, one wearing a vest covered in badges, raised their glasses. "To Noah!"

"Trying to work, Frank," Noah growled. And she swore his cheeks turned pink. His grip tightened around the third drink and she wondered if the martini glass's delicate stem would snap. But instead the tension rippled up his arm to his bicep. The muscle bulged and the red "Semper Fi" tattooed on his arm expanded.

"Sore subject?" She rested her elbows on the section of bar designated for the waitresses to pick up drinks. "Dominic bristles when people try to give him a pat on the back too."

"Yeah?" He remained focused on the last of the cocktails she'd ordered.

She nodded. "He says some of the things he's done don't deserve a toast. And recognizing that keeps him closer to the good-guy side of the murky grey space between ISIS evil and hero."

"Dominic said all that, huh? When was the last time you saw your brother?"

"Three years ago. He stopped by Portland while home on leave," she admitted. "But we email."

He shifted the drink to her end of the bar. "Wasn't sure you knew how, seeing as you never wrote back to me."

"You ran out of that barn . . ." She loaded the drinks onto her tray. "You wrote a long, drawn-out apology. But I wasn't sorry. I've made a lot of stupid choices, especially in high school." She looked up at him, straight into his blue eyes. "That night wasn't one of them."

Now, if she landed back in his barn, naked and ready to hand over her heart a second time, *that* would be a mistake.

He shook his head and a patron called for a beer. "Planning to tell Dominic that you're working here?"

"There's plenty I don't share with my brother."

"Like why you need the money?" he asked, his expression still set to doom and gloom.

"That too." She picked up the tray and walked away, praying it wouldn't spill. She made it to the booth and served the drinks. The blonde girl who'd turned twenty-one last week—Josie had checked her ID when she'd ordered, seeing as the bouncers didn't arrive until eight—handed her an extra five bucks.

Josie smiled as she turned and headed to the next table. So her feet hurt. And her boss was asking questions she'd rather not answer. This wasn't anything she couldn't handle. And maybe the next time she placed a drink order, she could convince Noah to smile.

"What can I get for you?" she asked, slipping the five-dollar bill into the Big Buck's apron with the rest of her tips and retrieving her notepad.

"How about your panties?" a deep, taunting voice said. "I've been waiting five long years to get my hands on them again."

She looked up and met Travis Taylor's smug smile. The past five years hadn't done him any favors. He'd gained a lot more than five pounds and none of his excess weight resembled muscle.

"My underwear isn't for sale," she said. But dammit, her voice wavered.

"Lost them in a hay wagon?" Travis teased.

"I can offer you drinks." Her pen was poised to take their order, her knuckles turning white from her death grip. "If you need ladies' undergarments, visit the Salem mall. Or is the state capital too far for you? Looks like you're still firmly planted in Forever."

"I've been waiting for you to come back from that fancy college of yours. But I never expected you to end up serving drinks," Travis said. "I just drove over here to see you. Your dad's been telling everyone about your homecoming. Word's spread like wildfire."

Her father had told everyone that she'd asked to stay in her old room? Forever's esteemed police chief hadn't even been home to greet her when she'd arrived. She'd driven around for more than an hour after her "job interview" with Noah. She'd wanted to arrive precisely at noon just like she'd told her dad over the phone on Sunday. But he'd already headed for the station, leaving behind a Post-it note and instruction on where to find the clean sheets.

"What do you want, Travis?" she demanded. "And your answer better be beer, wine, or liquor."

"Shots," he smirked. "A round of whiskey shots."

She turned and headed for the bar, counting her steps. *One, two, three...*

Steps four and five happened too fast to count. She slowed her pace, focused on her shoes. She refused to run from the man who'd wrapped his hands around her neck when she'd broken up with him five years ago. She'd dealt with a lot worse than Travis Taylor since then. His presence shouldn't shake her.

"Can you pour two shots of whiskey? I need to grab something from the back," she called to Noah as she walked past the bar.

Like my courage. I need a large dose fast if I'm going to serve Travis.

Noah's brow furrowed. "I'll get your shots. But don't take too long. We'll be slammed soon."

She nodded and pushed through the door into the peace and quiet of the back room. The door swung closed behind her, blocking out the dull roar of the Thursday crowd—and her scumbag ex. Cases of beer and booze lined the walls. A large metal desk covered in bills and other paperwork filled the far corner of the rectangular room. Another door stood at the back and led to a small rear parking lot. She was tempted to rush through the exit and escape into the night.

No. I can do this. I can go back out there and serve Travis without pouring his whiskey over his head.

She turned to face the door leading to the bar. She would march out there, serve her ex, and move on. Travis would not prevent her from landing this job. She would not let him ruin her trial shift. She refused—

The door swung open. She jumped back a step as her ragged nerves descended into chaos.

Noah peered through the open doorway. "You can come back out now. Travis is gone."

"You kicked him out?" she said as relief herded her wild nerves back into place. "You didn't need to—"

"He's not welcome here." Noah stepped into the room, allowing the door to close behind him as he crossed his arms in front of his chest. "It had nothing to do with you."

Her eyebrows shot up. Nothing to do with her? But then it dawned on her. She'd been gone for years. What if Travis had attacked someone else? And Noah had rushed to her rescue too.

"You're protecting someone—"

"No. I just don't want him here. My bar. My rules." He lowered his arms and turned to the door. "But he wasn't your only customer. There's a room full of people waiting on drinks out there. Are you ready to work, or did you change your mind about the job?"

"I'm ready." She followed him into the bar. "I'm not giving up because of Travis."

"Good."

And she caught a hint of his rare smile before he slipped back behind the bar.

She scanned the crowd and spotted a group of locals, men and women she recognized from high school, seated at an empty table. Withdrawing her notepad, she forced a smile and headed over. Travis had been right about one thing—word of her homecoming had spread. After she took their orders, politely avoiding their curious questions, she headed back to the bar.

"I bet your other new hires don't bring in this much business on their first shift," she said. "You should give me a cut of the profits from tonight."

Noah snorted. "Overreaching for someone who is auditioning for a full-time job."

She leaned over the bar, elbows resting on the wood. Her arms pushed her cleavage up and threatened to land her dress squarely in the indecent column. But she was still a long way from Hooters—and, hopefully, The Lost Kitten.

He glanced at her chest and she swore she saw a flash of heat in his eyes before he looked away.

Oh no. If he still wanted her, if that was his reason for pushing her away, for limiting her to a trial shift, and for kicking Travis out the door . . .

She straightened and smoothed her hands over her dress. One look at his supersized muscles and she wished she could explore beneath his shirt. She wanted to know what had changed—aside from his attitude—but she couldn't go there.

She needed a job and enough cash to break free from the past. Though one look at the gawking locals and she wondered if that was possible. Noah might have kicked Travis out, but it seemed as if the ghosts from Forever were hell-bent on haunting her.

Chapter Three

By NINE THIRTY, the university students had replaced the old-timers and locals. Noah kept an eye on the crowd as he worked. The bouncers had arrived at eight just before the crowd began to fill in for the DJ. An outside company handled the booking, and his rep there had assured him that the guy spinning tonight would appeal to the barely twenty-one crowd. Noah thought it sounded like the loud, repetitive stuff the guys he'd served with overseas played to pump up before heading out on patrol.

Damn war follows me everywhere.

He suspected the noise was part of the reason Chad and Lena had headed out to their truck. Lena, a West Point grad, had served two tours in Afghanistan, and now she relied on her service dog to navigate her PTSD. A bar overflowing with college kids and house music was too much for her. But Josh still hadn't turned up and they were determined to wait for the youngest Summers brother.

Noah handed over a beer with a forced smile and scanned the room for Josie. She'd looked ready to crumble after taking Travis's order. One glance at her pale face and Noah had been tempted to start a fight in his own bar. He'd told himself not to bother. He didn't need to play the hero. Not here. Not for her.

But he'd abandoned his post behind the bar and found himself at Travis's table by the time he'd finished telling himself to stay away. He'd threatened to break the other man's nose a second time if the lazy, unemployed ass didn't leave. Travis must have heard the rumors about Noah returning home unhinged and mad as hell, because Josie's ex had left. Sure, Travis had called him crazy. But the words had bounced off Noah as he'd headed for the back room.

Eyes on the busy bar, he caught sight of Josie. She was fighting her way through the mass of people with a tray of drinks for the corner booth. The crowd parted for her, the women offering a friendly smile and the guys—shit, they moved out of the way to get a better look at her curves. Even that black dress, better suited for an office than a bar, couldn't hide the fact that her breasts were fit for a fantasy.

Or maybe that was just his wicked imagination wanting something he couldn't have now that she was wearing a Big Buck's apron. Hell, these kids probably smiled at her just to be freaking nice to the woman distributing the drinks. He was the one who took one look at her chest and daydreamed about her breasts stripped free from that dress. And yeah, he was also the one who'd abandoned "nice" when he'd walked away from the marines.

He'd tried those first few months back. He'd smiled at every damn person in The Three Sisters. Most of the time. Once he'd walked away before getting his lunch. He'd bit his lip when men like Frank, who'd fought long before him, offered a simple thank you. Hell, he'd even tried flirting while volunteering at the Willamette Valley Gun Club. He'd dusted off his charm for Lena, pissing off both Chad and her service dog.

Now he didn't give a damn if everyone thought he was an ass. The things he'd done, the people he'd fought for, and the ones he'd been forced to call enemy had smashed his idea of good and bad. He lived in the grey area. Aside from keeping this bar running, a blow and a beer topped his list of wants.

Josie tapped a tipsy fool on the shoulder as she fought her way to her customers. Hell, he didn't want his best friend's little sister serving him a beer . . .

"Hey, man, I need three light beers. Whatever's cheap," a freckle-faced kid called.

Noah turned and retrieved the drinks. He set the bottles on the bar. And then it happened. One quick glance at Josie—because damn, he couldn't keep his eyes off her— and he saw a tall, built guy stumble right into Josie's filled tray. She fought to keep the cups balanced and failed. Three vodka tonics spilled down the front of her dress.

Noah moved to the side of the bar and lifted the slab of wood that separated his domain from the rest of the room.

"Hey, you didn't open these!" the guys who'd ordered the beers called out.

He didn't answer. He headed straight for Josie, pushing his way through the crowd. The jackass who'd pushed her had stumbled away. And she'd bent down to collect the cups on the ground.

"Leave it," he growled when he arrived at her side. "I'll send someone to pick it up."

"I can do it." She set the tray on the floor and reached for a plastic cup. As a rule, he stopped using the glassware after eight to avoid broken glasses everywhere. Also, he didn't have a dishwasher at the moment, which was starting to look like a damn good thing. If she'd been carrying glass . . . hell, he could picture broken pieces nestled between her breasts, cutting into her skin . . .

He took her arm and drew her up from the ground. "You're wet."

"And I smell like a vodka," she said with a laugh, holding the tray covered in empty cups. "Can you make new ones? Without charging them? I can cover the cost of the ones I spilled."

"They can wait for new drinks or go to the bar," he said as he led her through the crowd, toward the door to the back room. He pushed his way into the quiet storage area.

"Might lose them as customers," she said, her tone serious and easy to hear now with a wall between them and the music.

"I don't care." He headed for the row of four metal lockers by the desk. He opened the first door and withdrew a black T-shirt. "My dad kept a bunch of the old Big Buck Country Bar T-shirts."

"I don't need a shirt."

He turned and found her standing within arm's reach. The wet fabric clung to her chest, leaving the dress in the not-suitable-for-work column. Beer, vodka, tonic—he didn't give a damn what was spilled down her front. He wanted to lick her clean.

"Take the shirt," he said and he held it out to her. "Then you're free to go. I'll collect your pay from the register. All cash for the night."

"What about tomorrow night?" she demanded, taking the shirt from him. But she didn't move to put it on.

He hesitated. Part of him wanted her here, where he could watch over her, save her from anything and everything—including himself.

"I need this job, Noah," she added.

"You could find something else—"

"Because I spilled a few drinks?" Her voice was low and incredulous. "On my first night?"

Because I want you. Because I can't touch you if you work here. Because—

"Or because I took a minute to calm down so I wouldn't pour a shot of whiskey over my ex's head?" she demanded.

Noah let out a low laugh as the rush of adrenaline faded along with his need to save her. But his desire? It didn't budge. "If Travis comes back, you have my permission to pour a bottle over him."

"Does that mean I can keep the job? Because you promised to help me," she said. "Five years ago—"

"Sweetheart, I'm not that guy anymore." He looked her straight in the eye, daring her to look back and see *him*. Sure, he'd rushed to her rescue tonight. Twice. But he still wanted her. She should be off-limits, but the part of him that had come back from serving his country broken and jaded just didn't care.

"I don't need a hero," she shot back. "What I need is a friend willing to give me a job. I need the money."

"Maybe I can give you a loan," he said. Dammit, what was it about this woman that sent him spiraling into old habits, determined to look out for her?

Seeing all that determination to fight for what she needed—he remembered the teenager in the alley struggling against someone so much bigger. And he knew, he fucking *knew*, that fear lay on the other side of her resolve to fight. If her determination broke, the fear would surface. He might be an ass, but he couldn't walk away from Josie knowing she was afraid.

"No, it's too much," she said.

"How much do you owe, Josie?"

"Seventy thousand dollars," she said simply.

"What the—?" His eyes widened and he stepped back. "You planned to make that here?"

"I have a payment plan," she said. "Which is why I need a job."

And yeah, she was spelling it out for him as if he were a child. But how the hell had she saddled herself with so much debt?

"I thought you had a scholarship," he said.

"I don't have student loans." She bit her lower lip and

cocked her head. "Well, I do have some, but they're low and I've deferred payment for now."

"And you can't ask your dad?" He was still trying to wrap his head around the number she'd thrown out.

Seventy thousand dollars. Most people he knew didn't make anywhere close to that in a year, or even two.

She shook her head. "This is my responsibility."

Why? He needed to know. He had to find out what the hell had happened to Dominic's little sister, to the girl he'd thought about for the past five years, hoping like hell she was happy, or at least safe. But hearing that number—something had gone very, very wrong. While he'd been off fighting for his country, for Caroline, for a damn paycheck, Josie had landed herself in trouble.

"The job is yours," he said. And yeah, he had a sinking feeling those words would come back to bite him. "If you tell me who you owe."

"You can't tell Dominic," she said fiercely. "Or anyone else."

He nodded and hoped like hell she didn't make him say the words. He couldn't promise until he knew how she'd landed in this mess.

"I owe the hospital in Portland and a team of doctors." Her voice wavered, but she held his gaze.

"For what?" His imagination pieced together parts of an imaginary puzzle. Had she been in an accident? Had someone hurt her?

"Keeping my baby alive for twenty-seven days."

"Ah, Josie." He wanted to reach for her and wrap his

arms around her. But he could see her determination eroding. If he pulled her close, she might crumble. And he had a feeling that she needed every ounce of strength right now. "I didn't know . . ."

That she'd been pregnant. And not a soul in this gossip-crazy small town had breathed a word about her losing a child.

"No one did. I didn't even tell my father I was having a baby." She let out a sharp laugh. "I was planning on it. But then Matt, the guy I was seeing, left."

He felt a rush of white-hot anger so damn potent that he would have killed, with his bare hands, the man who'd abandoned Josie. Sweet Jesus, if he'd known . . . But what could he have done from halfway around the world? Hell, he'd been stationed with Caroline and in the end he hadn't been able to save her.

"If I came home pregnant and alone, I'd just confirm everyone's opinion that I'm a wild screwup." She spoke quickly as tears filled her eyes and rolled down her cheeks. But she didn't look away.

"College was my shot to prove them wrong," she continued. "So I stayed in school. I tried to do everything right. Prenatal vitamins. Organic food even though it cost so much more. I got a babysitting job. And I applied for Medicare. I hadn't bothered with insurance before. I was healthy. But then my water broke and there was nothing they could do to stop the labor. And he wasn't ready. My baby was just too early."

"I'm so sorry," he said. The words sounded hollow and insufficient. His friend's little sister, a woman who'd been his friend and, hell, even his lover for one brief night, she'd given birth alone. And she'd watched her baby die surrounded by hospital staff.

"But you understand why I need the money." She swiped at the tears as if determined to press forward. "My world stopped when my water broke, when he was born and he couldn't breathe. And everything crumbled when he died. There was nothing I could do for him. But I can do this. I can pay back the hospital and doctors who gave me twenty-seven days with him."

"Yes, you can," he said.

"Thank you." She lowered her chin to her chest and let the tears flow.

Hero or not, he was going to fight like hell for her. He'd known it before the first tear fell. But this time he was stepping into the fight with a big fat failure on his record. When he'd jumped to Josie's aid in the alley, he'd known he would win. But now? He didn't have a clue how to erase the grief and pain. He wasn't sure how to help her earn that kind of money.

"The job is yours, Josie," he said gruffly. "For as long as you need it."

And that was all he could promise.

JOSIE FOUGHT THE tears. He'd given her what she needed—a job. She'd found a way to earn money that didn't involve babysitting. With her resume, and in the current job climate, it felt like a miracle.

But she'd secretly hoped to earn her position. Prove

herself. Instead, she'd hidden from her ex and spilled a tray of drinks followed by the truth. She told him about Morgan, the baby she'd named after her late mother when she still had a sliver of hope he'd survive.

And Noah had handed her the job.

"I should get out there," she said, and by some miracle her voice sounded even, almost normal.

"You don't have to finish your shift. Your dress is still wet and . . ."

"And I look like I've been crying? I can fix my makeup in the bathroom. Plus, you handed me a new waitress uniform." She held up the shirt and forced a smile.

"No." He shook his head. "I gave you something to cover you up when you walked to your car."

"But it's crowded out there." She pulled the shirt over the vodka-soaked material clinging to her boobs like a second skin. She tied the excess fabric in a knot at her back. The T-shirt looked cute, as if she'd planned a retro look with a black miniskirt.

"We'll manage," he said. "You can come back tomorrow."

"But I'm here now." She placed her hands on her hips. Sparring with him felt good. In the past eighteen months since she'd left the intensive care unit to bury her baby instead of raise him, she'd discovered she could only stomach so much pity. She didn't want any more than he'd already offered—a simple "I'm sorry." Pity didn't change the past or pay her bills.

"It's only what, ten o'clock?" she continued. "You have hours before closing."

"That T-shirt will be soaked through soon," he countered.

"Damp. My dress was already beginning to dry. And maybe the customers will like seeing a picture of the old mechanical bull."

His gaze flickered to the picture on the T-shirt. "Most of the people out there never saw it in action."

But she had—the night she'd asked him to show her how to ride it. Sometimes she still dreamed about the feel of the bull moving beneath her, about Noah moving inside her . . .

A knock sounded at the back door before she could find her next comeback. She'd been close to marching off to the bathroom, reapplying her makeup, and returning to work. They could argue while she served drinks and collected tips.

"Noah?" The back door opened and Chad Summers poked his head inside.

"Yeah?" Noah called as he walked past her, heading for the rear exit.

The door swung wide and Chad stepped in, followed by another man. They had the same facial features and tall, muscular builds, but the second man was fair-skinned with bright red, curly hair.

"Sorry to interrupt." Chad cast a curious glance at her. "But Josh just arrived. He was held up because he offered to swing by a tract of private land Moore Timber plans to clear-cut. And he found a woman camping out. No car. Just a sleeping bag and pack."

Josh nodded and his red curls fell across his forehead. "I approached her and, dude, I could tell she'd been living out there for a while. When I talked to her, and basically told her she needed to leave before the crew moved in to harvest, hell, I half expected her to be one of those crazy environmentalists. But she said she was searching for a friend. Before she'd tell me a name, she made me swear I wouldn't breathe a word to anyone. And shit, at this point, I was ready to the call the police. She seemed nuts. But then she said she was looking for you."

"What's her name?" Noah demanded.

"Caroline," Josh said. "I told her I knew you. I offered to give you a call. But she started to gather her bag. Said she couldn't trust anyone. Claimed someone was after her and they would come after you too. She told me she had to warn you."

"Shit," Noah cursed.

Josie turned to him. She'd been inching back, prepared to sneak away and finish her shift while Noah informed the Summers brothers that they'd found some crazy chick in the woods.

"So you know her?" Chad jumped in.

"Yeah. And if she says someone if coming for us, she's probably right," Noah said. "Where is she now? Did you give her a ride?"

Josh shook his head. "No offense, Noah, but I didn't believe her story. I went to get my cell from my truck to call you and when I turned back, she'd vanished. Just slipped away without a sound."

"Caroline's a marine," Noah said as he withdrew his truck key. "She's fast and quiet. Trust me, I served with her."

"A marine," Chad said. "Present tense?"

"Yes," Noah said. "And I need to find her."

Chapter Four

THE SMELL OF stale beer and a ray of sunlight packed a powerful punch first thing in the morning. Josie opened her eyes to both and wished she hadn't slept in the old Big Buck's shirt that she'd worn for the rest of her shift—after Noah had slipped out to search for the mysterious Caroline.

She glanced at the window. The white curtains her mother had picked out welcomed the early-morning light instead of blocking it out.

"I should have asked for blackout drapes," she muttered. But at five years old she'd risen with the sun.

"Josie?" Her dad's booming voice called from the other side of her door. "Are you awake?"

"Yes." She tossed off the covers and slid out of bed. Thinking about her mom, about how much she'd needed her these past few years, would only lead to tears. "I'm up."

"I'm making eggs before I head back to the station," her father announced.

"I'll be right down." She opened her duffel bag and riffled through it, searching for a pair of pants and a clean shirt. She couldn't sit down to breakfast with the chief of police smelling like she'd rolled in booze last night.

She walked into the farmhouse kitchen wearing sweatpants and an old tank top. Her father stood by the stove, his gaze focused on a frying pan. With the build of a professional linebacker, her dad looked like a cartoon character wearing an apron and holding the spatula in one hand.

"Morning, Dad." She moved around the familiar space, pouring juice and setting the four-top wooden table. "Thank you for letting me stay here."

"It's your home." Her father turned from the stove with two plates of scrambled eggs layered with cheese and herbs. "I would have been here yesterday, but Lewis, he's my new deputy, his wife just had a baby."

"I managed just fine," she said as he set a plate in front of her. She missed her father's cooking. After the morning sickness and the initial oh-shit-I'm-having-a-baby panic faded, she'd dreamed about coming home and eating at this table. But she'd dreaded the conversation that would follow when he saw her belly. He'd grounded her through half of high school only for her to show up pregnant once she went to college?

Dad, I think you were right about me. I think this whole town was right. I'm always going to be the girl who needs saving, the one who's not strong enough to take care of herself.

No, she couldn't say those words. So she'd tried to manage on her own. And still failed. She hadn't been strong enough. Not even close.

"I saw your note," he said as he claimed the seat across from her. "You're working at Big Buck's?"

"Noah gave me a job."

"He's a good kid. And he's doing a fine job with that bar." He stabbed his fork into the eggs. "It's a big relief for his father having him home. Buck fell a few months ago helping his neighbor set a hunting stand up in a tree. He broke his leg and now he's having a hard time getting around, from what I hear. Good thing his son had come home by then."

She nodded and focused on eating. Was her father waiting for Dominic to come back? It didn't seem likely now that he'd gone through Ranger School. He might have left for basic training at the same time as Noah—and Ryan, the third in their trio—but she suspected her brother was the only one who wanted to be there.

She glanced up from her half-empty dish. The sound of their forks on the plates filled the otherwise empty kitchen.

"I'm glad you're home," her father said suddenly. "But if you came back because . . . If there is something wrong, I'd like to know. I want to help."

Where do I begin?

"I just needed a job and a fresh start," she said.

She couldn't tell the man who'd spent years questioning

her choices about the baby. He'd been right every time. But choosing the wrong guy and losing a baby? This wasn't a mark on her record. It was an F for "failure." It had broken her heart in ways she hadn't imagined possible. She'd held herself accountable. She couldn't bear to add his judgment too. Not yet.

"WAITING FOR THE cases of beer to count themselves?" Josie asked as she pushed through the door leading to Big Buck's back room and headed for Noah. He looked like he hadn't slept since the night the Summers brothers launched the hunt for the mysterious Caroline.

Four days had passed since her trial shift and Josie hadn't learned anything more about the missing marine. But she knew Noah had made it his mission to find her. He was either serving drinks, searching the Willamette Valley for Caroline, or trying to do the inventory when he was too tired to count.

He glanced at her and then turned his attention back to the cases neatly stacked by the back wall. "This new citrus summer ale doesn't sell. I still have . . . so damn much."

"Five cases." She reached out and took the clipboard and pen from his hands. She hadn't slept much either between working through the weekend at the bar and getting up in the morning for awkward breakfasts with her father. But she'd rested long enough to count boxes. Unlike her boss. She scrolled down the list, found the summer ale, and wrote the number.

"Cases of this stuff and everyone wants Fern's Hoppy Heaven IPA," he muttered.

"So get that instead." She scanned the rows of beer boxes before adding a few zeros to the inventory list. "And we also need light beer."

"Only a few bars in Portland have the Hoppy Heaven on draft," he said. "A bunch of the students drive up to the brewery once a week to buy a four-pack. An hour's drive to buy four cans of beer and they have to wait in line when they get there." He shook his head. "I need to convince the brewery to let us sell it here."

"I could help you," she said, scribbling another zero on the inventory sheet. "I could take over the ordering."

"Four shifts in and you're trying for a promotion?" Noah said.

"Only if it pays more." She moved to the kegs and bent over one to read the label. She scribbled another number on the list and waited for him to say something. Maybe a sharp "Not going to happen" or "It doesn't pay a penny more."

Silence.

"Not that I'm complaining," she continued. "The tips have been great. It probably helps that I haven't spilled a single drink since that first night." She glanced up to see if he'd fallen asleep standing up staring at the beer.

Nope, still awake. And not looking at the beer. Not unless he expected to find a bottle buried between her breasts.

"I'm not hiding a can of that super special IPA down my shirt," she teased as she stood up. "But you can stare at my cleavage all you want. Nothing is going to happen."

Noah looked up from her chest and raised an eyebrow. "Never writing back to me, did that help you forget about the night you rode the bull?"

"No," she said firmly. "I didn't want to forget. Maybe take back what I said. But now . . . I can't take another ride with you."

"You're sure about that?" he asked mildly. But she saw the tension rippling through his muscles. This man was close to falling asleep on his feet. But Noah still looked as if he would toss her over his shoulder and carry her straight to his barn.

Do it!

She felt the desire rising up and leaving her wanting what she couldn't have—him.

"I'm sure," she said softly.

Because no matter how much I want to touch you, I'm terrified one kiss, one wild night, will damage what's left of my heart.

But she wasn't going to spell out her feelings and fears for him. As much as she hated living with fear, she wasn't going to present a challenge or give him a chance to prove that sometimes desire trumped everything else. Because, oh God, if her longing for Noah and his supersized muscles won . . .

"Nothing will happen," she continued. "Because I have a history of only falling for total jerks."

"I can be a jerk," he said, his tone daring her to prove him wrong as he crossed his arms in front of his chest. His muscles flexed and his Semper Fi tattoo stared back at her as if the marines motto translated into "Bad Boy Material."

"I'm sure you can," she said. But she knew better than to travel down that road. She moved to his side and patted his arm. He stared down at her hand as if she'd seared the blond hair. She withdrew her hand and added, "I just want you to know it won't be a problem."

"The other night, while you were working your first shift, I wanted to lick the vodka off your breasts." He spoke in a low tone and his gaze met hers. The look in his eyes screamed *I dare you to pat me like a freaking puppy again.*

"You wouldn't try now that I'm full-time." Her statement hovered close to question-mark territory.

"Get a bottle and try me," he said. "I'll probably break my own damn rule about fooling around with the employees."

Her hand itched to reach for the nearest liquor bottle. But she was too much of a coward. Plus, she didn't think he would do it. She knew jerks, the kind of men who hit, the ones who left, and the guys who didn't give a damn. Becoming a marine, deploying to Afghanistan, fighting—the experience had knocked the pedestal of perfection right out from under him. But that didn't make him a jerk. Just a good man who'd gone to war and come home a little lost. A former soldier who'd rather give in to desire instead of face his own demons.

She stared at the lines around his eyes. Right now, he looked every inch a good guy who'd rather use her breasts as a pillow instead of a shot glass.

"Maybe later. You're tired," she said. "Let me finish the inventory while you rest."

He shook his head. "I'm fine. I've gone days with only an occasional combat nap."

"This isn't a war zone," she said softly. "Just because you're searching for someone . . . it's not the same."

He stared at her as if ready to argue. "No, it's not," he said finally. "Just one big Goddamn nightmare."

"Maybe Caroline left," she said. *And took the nightmare with her.*

"No."

She knew he was right. Problems didn't just fade away. And the nightmares stayed whether you slept or not.

"If you're planning to comb through the woods again tonight," she said, knowing he would, "you should rest. Take a combat nap. Maybe make this one a double while I finish up here."

"I could use a few minutes of shut-eye," he admitted. "I have a meeting with Fern's Brewery in the morning. Think you can be accurate with the list?"

"Don't worry, I've been counting since grade school," she said, making a mental note to attend the meeting with him. He'd been joking about a promotion. But one day soon he might need an assistant manager to handle the ordering. And before she had dropped out of college, she'd been on her way to earning a degree in business management and marketing.

"When is the meeting?" she asked.

"Nine," he said with a sigh. "But they're located up near Portland. Long drive."

"I could drive," she offered. "And you could sleep along the way."

"Jesus, you really are angling for a promotion, aren't you," he said.

"Is that a yes?"

"I'll think about it." Then he turned to the door. "I'm going to crash in my truck. Wake me before we open."

Chapter Five

Wake up, Sleeping Beauty.

The memory of her soft voice floated through his dream. Hours earlier, before the sun sank behind the mountains for the night, Josie had knocked on his truck window. He'd been locked in a dreamscape filled with one boom after another—an attack so vivid he could almost smell the burning canvas of the tent the insurgents had managed to hit with the rocket fire. Caroline had been by his side, shouldering an M16 while wiping away tears . . .

Caroline.

Noah opened his eyes and stared out into the bright morning sky. Right now, Josie wasn't standing outside his truck ready to drag his ass into the bar when all he wanted to do was pull her in and lose himself in her soft curves. To hell with the fact she worked for him. To hell with Dominic and the shit storm he'd rain down on

Noah for laying a finger on his sister. To hell with the last five years.

He ran a hand over his face. Sometimes he wished he'd never left the barn that night five years ago. If he could have stayed there with Josie, keeping everyone else on the other side . . . but damn, he couldn't live the rest of his life believing he could save the world. Tonight marked night five and he couldn't even find the one person he wanted to help.

Last night, after he'd followed Josie into the bar—which she'd set up for the busy shift *after* she'd completed his inventory and done a helluva lot better job than he could have—he'd endured hours of watching her move and smile at the customers. He'd closed up early and then, he'd gone to meet up with Josh Summers. Together, they'd searched another section of Oregon timber country for Caroline, who sure as shit acted like she didn't want to be found. He'd driven home close to dawn, parked his truck beside the barn, and rested his eyes for a minute. That minute had extended until the memory of Josie woke him, sporting a whole world of wanting.

He adjusted himself and opened the truck door. As he stepped down, he glanced at the barn. Shit, the light was on again. Had his father wandered out? Not likely. His old man had a hard time navigating the gravel separating the house from the barn with the walker the doctors had insisted he use after the fall. And they didn't keep animals in there anymore. Too much work.

The side door opened before he reached the structure and a familiar face peered out.

"Caroline?" He stopped four feet from the barn and stared. "How the hell—"

"I had your address," she said, her voice soft. Her mouth formed a thin line. Freckles dotted her nose, suggesting her fair skin had been exposed to the elements for a while. And her long dark hair, which he'd grown accustomed to being pulled back in a tight bun, now flowed loose around her shoulders. He didn't know much about women's hair, but he knew she needed a brush, and maybe a pair of scissors.

She wore black pants, a baggy black T-shirt, and combat boots. The clothes were three, maybe four sizes too large for her frame. Between Caroline's height—she stood roughly as tall as Josie—and her delicate girl-next-door features, she'd always looked like she belonged in Disney World playing a fairy-tale princess, not in the US Marine Corps.

"So you walked here from where?" he asked, focusing his sleep-deprived brain. He moved closer to her, but stayed out of arm's reach. He wanted to offer her the illusion of safety. He couldn't make promises, but he doubted there were threats hiding in the barn. He'd been home for months and the only things he'd found were some old furniture, the mechanical bull, and memories.

"I was staying with my sister in Northern California. But he found me," she said.

"Dustin?" he asked.

"Yes. He showed up and threatened to turn me in." Her tone was devoid of drama as if she expected to open the door and find her rapist on her doorstep.

"Did he hurt you?" he asked, not that it would change a damn thing. If he saw their former commanding officer again nothing would hold him back. He wouldn't wait for justice. He'd beat the crap out of Dustin.

She shook her head. "He didn't touch me. But he said he was planning to call the police."

And when they found her they'd hand her over to the military. She'd probably face jail time for her unauthorized absence. It wouldn't matter that she'd run because she couldn't face serving alongside men who'd fought at her side one minute, placing their lives in her hands, and threatened her the next. And if she had returned, serving with those men would be pure hell because she'd accused one of them—their leader—of rape. She'd gotten their commanding officer kicked out of the marines because she'd had a witness willing to testify.

Him.

"So you ran," he said.

"I needed to find you," she said. "Dustin's pissed at me. But he blames you for losing his career. His wife left him and—we should move inside."

Caroline scanned the house and the drive, showing a hint of fear for the first time. He knew his dad wouldn't wake for a few hours. And he was familiar with the sounds—cars speeding over the dirt road, the neighbor's rooster, who operated on the assumption that it was always rise-and-shine time—but she clearly viewed them as potential threats.

"Sure," he said and followed her into the old, mostly empty barn. The hay bales had disappeared years ago, but otherwise the space looked pretty much the same. Old boxes, some tools, a rusted gate, and a collection of broken furniture that belonged in the dump.

He left the door open behind them, allowing a beam of light to slip in and illuminate the mechanical bull in the corner surrounded by faded red, white, and blue cushions. His dad had thrown an old western saddle over the bull's back. Now the damn thing looked like it wanted to go for a ride even though it probably hadn't been turned on since he'd left for basic training.

He followed Caroline into the light and over to the pads surrounding the bull. A backpack rested on the edge, packed and ready to go. It was the only sign she'd been staying in his barn.

"How long have you been here?" he asked. "After you talked to Josh Summers, hell, I've been out looking for you every night."

"Yesterday afternoon," she said. "I wasn't sure I could trust Josh. He started talking about how they needed to start clearing the land. And he mentioned the police would be called in to remove anyone found on the premises. So I slipped away when he went to get his phone."

"He thought you were trying to save the trees," he said. "But Josh is a good guy. He just thought it sounded a little nuts when you claimed someone was after you."

"Dustin wants revenge," she said simply. "He thinks you stole a lot from him."

"He took a helluva lot more from you," he said. "I remember, Caroline. Shit, I got up every night to walk you to the bathroom and make sure he wouldn't find you alone in the dark again and take what he wanted even if you made it clear you weren't interested. If Dustin shows up here, I'm going to start throwing punches before he says a word. Do you have any idea how badly I wanted to hit him when he tossed out those degrading commands? Every damn time he ordered you to his bed in front of the guys, laughing it off a second later like it was one big joke?"

"I know," she said.

"If he shows ups here—"

"Noah?" Josie's voice came from the open doorway and he heard the sound of her shoes clicking on the barn's cement floor. What the hell was she doing in heels in his freaking barn?

Breathing life into my fantasies . . . Another ride on the bull. . .

But they had an audience and Josie was wearing the office-ready dress she'd worn for her first shift at the bar.

"I heard your voice," Josie said. She came to a halt and looked past him. The sunlight formed a halo around her as she slowly raised her hands, palms up in a show of surrender.

"And you must be Caroline," she added, looking past him. "Please don't shoot."

Chapter Six

As a rule, Josie usually forgot to feel fear until it was too late. Her ex-boyfriend had towered over her, her cheek still stinging from the smack of his palm, and she'd thought, *I'm going to kick the shit out of him.* The fear hadn't seeped in until after Noah had chased him away.

But staring down a wild-haired woman sporting a wood-nymph-meets–GI Jane look, complete with the gun pointed at her, and Josie's fear rose fast and furious. Her heart pounded and she couldn't for the life of her tell if she was still breathing.

"You can put the gun down," Josie said. "I work for Noah. The assistant manager at Big Buck's." Oh, she was definitely landing a promotion out of this mess. "We're going to Portland to—"

"Caroline," Noah said, his voice surprisingly calm as he stepped in front of the gun-wielding woman he'd spent the past five nights searching for in the woods. "Put the gun down."

She stopped breathing this time. No question about it. Every muscle in her body begged to move, run in front of Noah, save him—and stay frozen all at the same time. It felt as if her brain had gone haywire and started sending out mixed signals. *Go! Stay! Save Noah!*

"Please, Caroline," he added.

Ms. Crazy-Hair GI Jane lowered her arms and tucked the gun into the waist of her cargo pants. But she didn't offer a *sorry, I forgot I wasn't supposed to shoot Noah's employees in his barn.*

Of course, if Josie had gone to war and been attacked by the good guys, she'd probably keep a gun or two in her pants as well. She'd heard enough while walking up to the barn to piece together why Caroline had come looking for Noah. He'd been Caroline's hero when she needed one most.

Welcome to the club, GI Jane.

Josie looked past Caroline to the mechanical bull. The last time she'd seen that bull, it had been wearing her dress and spinning to a slow, sensual beat while she lay naked on the padding below. And Noah had just walked out the door to greet her brother . . .

Did Caroline belong to the naked-bull-riding-with-Noah club too? He would jump to a woman's defense even if she wasn't *his*. But she'd also bet the marine looked pretty with her hair brushed. Pretty and kind of like Josie's more athletic twin in a strange way.

Not that it mattered. Noah wasn't hers. And from the sounds of it, Caroline had much bigger problems than whether Noah wanted to take her for a naked ride, on his bull or anywhere else. Problems Caroline had delivered straight to Noah's doorstep.

"I need to go to this meeting," he said to Caroline. "But I'd like you to stay. My dad's up at the house. I'll take you up and introduce you before I head out. And we'll lock up that gun."

Caroline pushed her hair out of her face. "I'd love a shower. But I need—"

"You'll get the gun back," he promised. "But tonight. After we've had a chance to talk and determine your next step."

Caroline let out a brittle laugh. "I've just been trying to get from one day to the next and not burn through all the money my sister gave me too fast."

"Take a shower, rest, and we'll talk," Noah said as he walked over and picked up her backpack. He let her keep the gun, Josie noted as they headed past her. She followed them out into the parking area.

"Josie, wait here. I'll be right back," Noah said, glancing at her over his shoulder.

She nodded and turned to her car. Her heart rate had slowed after Caroline lowered the gun, but it wasn't anywhere close to normal. Not yet. She'd landed herself in stupid situations before. But a gun pointed at her? That was a first.

But it had almost been worse seeing it directed at Noah.

Fifteen minutes later, Noah walked down the porch steps and headed over to her. "Let's go. You're driving so I can sleep. Consider it part of the assistant manager job."

"So I get the promotion?" She followed him to her red Mini and opened the driver's side door. "And a raise?"

"Don't say a word about Caroline, and yeah, I'll bump up your hourly." He opened the passenger side door and settled all six-foot plus of his muscular body into her compact car. Thank goodness she'd unloaded most of her belongings at her dad's place.

"I won't tell a soul." She buckled her seat belt. "I mean if word got out about how you helped Caroline no one would ever buy your I'm-a-surly-jerk routine again."

"You heard a helluva lot," he muttered.

"Enough." She slid the key into the ignition.

"Look," he said, turning his head to face her. "A lot of people wouldn't agree with what I did. Testifying against my commanding officer. The marines are like a band of brothers. And I broke that bond. But if I hadn't said something, it would have been her word against Dustin's and he claimed he never touched her. My testimony proved otherwise and he changed his story to an affair, pretending she'd consented to sleep with him. And after all that, they expected her to go back and finish her term of service alongside some of the other guys who'd harassed her."

"What?" she said. Seeing Caroline now, it was hard to believe anyone would march up to her and demand the she continue to serve. She wasn't sure Caroline should be allowed to have a weapon, never mind defend their country. "How could they?"

"The men we served with haven't done anything wrong. I watched her fight alongside these guys, driving them around and getting shot at, only to return to the base and become the butt of their jokes. In the beginning, she played along, trying to be one of the group. And I did too, laughing at some things that were pretty damn inappropriate. But over time, it crossed a line and turned into harassment."

"She couldn't do anything?" She felt a large dose of outrage on behalf of the woman who'd pulled a gun on her earlier.

"Against a few good soldiers? That defense still holds a lot of weight, especially when you're talking about what looks like a grey area. Hell, the only way Caroline got anywhere with her rape case against our commanding officer was because I testified. And even then, Dustin was acquitted for rape. He received a dishonorable discharge for adultery. He was married at the time, and not to Caroline."

"That's awful."

"Yeah." He turned his head and stared straight out the window. "But that's how it is. Being a marine doesn't make a man a hero. I served with plenty of good men and women who deserved the label for their actions. Take away the label—soldier, sailor, Special Forces, whatever—and put them in those same situations and they'd still be heroes."

"You are too," she said firmly.

"No, I just did my job, which sucked half the time because it turns out I like shooting at paper targets, not people. And I took a lot of shit for who I chose to defend." He leaned his head back and closed his eyes. "Planning to start this car anytime soon?"

She turned the key. The car sputtered and made a clicking noise. And then nothing. "Shoot."

He opened one eye. "Is this toy going to get us there?"

"It's temperamental." She turned the key and this time it worked. "See? Fine now."

"Uh-huh," he murmured. "To be clear, I don't know how to fix this thing if it breaks down between here and Portland."

"I do. As long as we don't need a new part. Dominic taught me. But nothing is going to happen today." She glanced over at Noah as she reached the top of the drive. He'd already drifted off to sleep. The facial muscles he tried to force into a scowl instead of his breathtaking smile appeared relaxed.

He's so damn sexy when he sleeps.

"You're a good man," she whispered as she turned out of his drive. "I know you are, Noah."

NOAH COULD HAVE slept for a week. But they reached the brewery in a little over an hour. The owner and brewmaster had started the meeting with a solid "never," as in Big Buck's would not sell the West Coast's hottest beer in this lifetime. But after talking to Josie and hearing her spout numbers as if she'd memorized his books for the last month, the owner had warmed to her suggestions.

Hell, maybe she had memorized the books and analyzed the numbers in her spare time. Back in high school, she'd earned a full ride to college. Noah knew they didn't hand those out lightly. He'd led his football team to state, but he'd never come close to four free years at a top-tier university.

Part of him hated the fact that her education was derailed. She could have done a helluva lot more than win over the head of Oregon's trendiest brewery. But Noah wasn't about to complain. He'd spent years fighting to keep Big Buck's afloat. And Josie had turned the brewmaster's "never" into a one big "yes." They wanted the new IPA all the college students drove over an hour to purchase because no one carried it in their area? Done. The pale ale too? Not a problem.

An hour later, he followed a triumphant Josie back to her Mini.

"You did a great job," he said, climbing into her clown car. "Earned that assistant manager position and the right to work with any of the other local breweries directly from here on out."

"Thank you," she said. "I enjoy serving drinks, but taking meetings and negotiating? It feels great to go in there and win."

And I'm so damn glad I could give that to you.

She put her car in reverse, her movements swift and self-assured. Did she have a clue how her confidence spoke to the parts of his anatomy that had no business responding to his employee's victory? After all she'd been through, Josie hadn't lost her drive. This wasn't a woman who played the victim. She pushed through, fighting her way back.

I'm proud of you, Josie.

But hell, if he said those words she'd probably demand another raise.

"I'm planning to sleep on the drive back," he said. And God help him if he started dreaming about her. He had a feeling his mind would head straight for inappropriate with the woman who'd just proven to be his most valuable employee.

"I won't bother you," she promised. "But I have one question first."

"Shoot."

"Is there any reason Caroline can't work for you?" she asked.

"What?" he said.

"You need a dishwasher, especially on the busy nights. It wouldn't pay much. But it would be something," she continued if he wasn't staring at her profile trying to figure out if he'd missed something. The nap on the way down had helped his sleep-deprived mind. But after working and worrying twenty-four/seven for five days, he needed a solid five or six hours before he felt fully functional.

"So any reason she can't join the Big Buck's team?" she asked, glancing at her blind spot as she merged onto the highway.

He grinned and shook his head. Yesterday, he'd told her he had a rule against dating his employees at the bar. And now she was asking . . .

His smiled widened. "You're fishing."

After five long days of torturing himself with images of Caroline dead in the woods, or injured and alone, after six days of working with Josie, knowing she'd come to him for help after losing her child, and facing the fact that he still wanted her, she wished to know if he'd slept with Caroline. All the pain and mental torture of the past few days, all the hard facts, had been reduced to a question innocent seventh graders asked each other: Do you like her?

"Yes." She glanced over at him.

"Thinking about taking me up on the offer to lick you clean?" he asked mildly.

She let out a laugh and then fell silent. Finally, she said, "I want to help Caroline."

"So you're looking out for the woman who tried to shoot you earlier?"

The color faded from her cheeks. "She wasn't going to discharge her weapon."

Probably not, but Caroline had still scared the hell out of him.

"You've been searching for her after work," she said. "I know you want to help her."

"I do," he admitted. "And now that I've taken on more management, I'm thinking about relaxing some of the rules."

"Oh," she said. "Really?"

"Like maybe I could pay one very part-time, temporary employee off the books and in cash."

"That's not the rule I was talking about and you know it," she said.

Yeah, he knew. But he couldn't resist the urge to tease her.

"Plus you paid me in cash out of the register that first night," she added.

"I'm thinking about relaxing the other rules too."

But not because Caroline showed up.

He leaned his head back, knowing he needed another combat nap or he'd fall asleep standing up at work tonight. He closed his eyes and prepared to drift off into a dream that might become a reality—if he meant what he'd said about relaxing his rule. Sure, Dominic would still kick the shit out of him if he ever made his way back to Oregon. And after losing her baby, suffering a breakup with her asshole ex, Josie might be looking for a helluva lot more than Noah could deliver.

He frowned. She deserved a lot after all she'd been through. What had she said yesterday? *Look all you want, I don't fall for the good guys?* But he wasn't a saint. Not even close. If she accepted that, then maybe a night or two—

"I just wanted to know if Caroline was part of your naked-bull-riding club," Josie murmured. "If her membership might be current."

"No. We were never involved," he said without opening his eyes. "And for the record, sweetheart, you're the only member of that club."

Chapter Seven

"I HEAR YOUR staffing criteria has shifted from experienced bartenders to women who need a job." Chad Summers walked up to the nearly empty bar twenty minutes after noon on Friday.

Noah glanced at the door to the back room. Josie was in there teaching Caroline how to use the commercial dishwasher, a skill Josie herself had only picked up a few days ago. The two women got along just fine now that he'd erased Josie's concern that he'd been naked bull riding, or naked anything else, with Caroline.

And it probably helped that Caroline had taken a shower. Plus, his fellow marine had agreed to let him keep her gun in his safe. He just hoped they didn't break the dishwasher during the lesson or he'd be serving everyone in plastic cups until he could replace it.

"They're not pouring shots and mixing drinks," Noah said.

"Yet," Chad said.

"Yet," Noah agreed. "What can I get for you?"

Moore Timber's number one helicopter pilot pointed to Fern's Hoppy Heaven, the special IPA half the country had stopped by to sample yesterday. At this rate, they'd need another keg by tomorrow. "I hear Josie helped you get that crazy beer. Pretty damn impressive for one of your strays."

"One of my what?" Noah set the beer in front of Chad.

"Elvira told everyone in the coffee line at The Three Sisters this morning about how you'd taken in two women desperate for work and given them jobs. She claims you have a heart of gold." Chad raised his glass. "All I can say is that it's a damn good thing I found Lena in my bed before she met you."

"Elvira's full of shit," Noah said and Chad laughed. Hell, they both knew that was a lie. He had a cocktail waitress with a week's experience who'd shown up on his doorstep damn near begging for the job. And a dishwasher who was wanted by the police. Plus, his former commanding officer might be hunting for Caroline. Oh, and she lived in his spare bedroom for now.

"Hey, Josh is planning to stop in later," Chad said after taking one long drink from his beer. "Can he slip into the back and talk to Caroline? He wanted to check in and apologize for mistaking her for a tree-hugger."

"Sure, though I don't think she took that as an insult."

Chad snorted. "It is to Josh."

Noah nodded. The men who'd built their lives around the timber industry, who took pride in caring for the land, harvesting and then replanting, they didn't exactly get along with the tree-huggers.

"After all the time Josh volunteered to the search, yeah he can head back when he gets here," Noah said. "But he can't see her alone."

"Of course." The door to the back room swung open and Josie walked in. Chad held up his beer. "To Josie, for making Big Buck's the only bar with Fern's Hoppy Heaven on tap outside of Portland!"

"To Josie!" a pair of college students echoed from the other end of the room.

She smiled and took a bow, then headed for the service side of the bar. He walked over to meet her. And yeah, his wide grin pretty much matched hers.

"You're not getting another raise," he said before she opened her mouth. She'd been angling for another increase since she'd witnessed the Hoppy Heaven's popularity.

She leaned over the counter. "How about a bonus for giving the customers something else to raise their glasses to?"

He crossed his arms in front of his chest and watched her gaze flicker to the tattoo on his bicep. Just for a second. Then she was staring back at him again, but he was the only one smiling like a fool. The challenge in her big green eyes erased the sullen mood she'd accused him of wearing like a cloak.

"I'll think about it," he said, flexing his arms. He hoped she wanted the kind of extra benefit he was thinking of offering her—a kiss that would prove she'd carried the memory of that night in the barn around with her too.

JOSIE HAD STOPPED writing down orders by seven that evening. Nearly everyone who walked into the bar asked for a Fern's Hoppy Heaven. And the few who requested a pop or a mixed drink, well, she'd gotten pretty good at remembering orders and linking faces with drinks.

One of the weekend bouncers had arrived early to help manage the crowd. She'd packed this place and secured her job. Noah wouldn't dare take it away from her now.

She'd walked out of that meeting at the brewery feeling as if she could do anything. She could run this bar, pay her bills, and even secure a job for a woman trying to find her way back from a hell Josie could only imagine.

And I could fight the fear holding me back from stealing a peek beneath Noah's Big Buck's T-shirt at the muscles he fine-tuned over the past few years.

A touch. A taste. Nothing serious. Nothing that might lead to more.

Well, physically she was ready. It had been almost two years since she'd had sex. But sex led to broken hearts. Especially sex with Noah. And if they messed up with the birth control—a baby.

She couldn't risk losing another child. It would break her. She wasn't strong enough. Not yet, when she hadn't even finished paying for the first loss. But even after she sent that last check, she knew the grief, the guilt, the feeling of failure, none of it would ever fully recede.

Still, a kiss, maybe two—that was different. She wasn't afraid of one simple kiss. OK, maybe a little scared that she might start to feel something for him the second his lips touched hers. But she didn't want to live in fear.

"Hey, Josie," Noah called from behind the bar. "Are you all right? Need a break?"

She turned to him and saw his furrowed brow. Concern shone in his blue eyes. "I'm fine," she said, knowing he'd vault over the bar if he thought she needed a full-blown rescue. But she didn't. Not this time.

Just a kiss to prove she was stronger than the imaginary demons trying to keep a hold on her. A kiss to prove the confident woman who walked into that meeting yesterday wasn't a mirage.

"Good. Then do you mind taking Josh back to see our new dishwasher? I'm swamped, but he wanted to say hi. And she might feel better if you're there," he called over the buzz of the crowd.

She nodded in agreement and scanned the people at the bar looking for the redheaded Summers brother. Josh waved and headed over.

"The woman of the hour," Josh said. "Congratulations on putting Big Buck's on the map for something other than a mechanical bull."

"That hasn't been here in years," she said, leading the way to the relative quiet of the back room.

"Wow," Josh said, drawing to a halt in the middle of the room. One glance at him, and Josie knew he wasn't staring at the row of kegs that had been delivered yesterday. He'd spotted Caroline slamming the dishwasher closed.

"Getting out of the woods looks good on you, Miss Caroline," he called.

Caroline turned and spotted Josh. She offered a tentative smile. "I'd been camping for a while when you found me," she admitted.

"I owe you an apology," he said. "I should have offered you a ride straight over to Big Buck's. To Noah. I'm sorry I didn't believe your story about someone being after you. I didn't realize you were a marine."

She took a step back and her hand moved to her waistband searching for the weapon thankfully locked in Noah's safe.

"Your secret is safe with me," Josh said, still beaming at Caroline as if the sight of a petite woman in combat boots, jean shorts, and an oversized Big Buck's shirt blew him away. "My short-term memory is still just starting to work again after a logging accident."

"I'm sorry," Caroline said. "About the accident."

Josh shrugged. "Sometime life delivers you a whole pile of shit and there's nothing you can do about it."

"Yes. It does." Caroline's arms dropped to her side.

"But at the end of the day, my siblings found a great doctor for me and I learned to bake an awesome pie while working on my memory." Josh rested an elbow on the stainless-steel counter beside the dishwasher. "Do you like pie, Caroline?"

"I do," she murmured.

"I'll bake one for you sometime." He stood and took a step back. "I'll let you ladies get back to work. But I'll see you soon, Miss Caroline. When I drop off your pie."

Josh headed for the swinging door. He gave Caroline one last wave and disappeared into the other room.

"I can't accept a pie from him," Caroline said. "Or eat one with him."

"If you give me a slice, I'll chaperone your pie-eating date," Josie volunteered.

The marine turned back to the dishwasher. "I can't."

"It's just dessert."

Caroline glanced over her shoulder. A hollow, haunted look had replaced her smile. "It's never just a pie."

"I know." One date, one dessert could stumble head-long into pain and heartache. And looking at the marine turned dishwasher, Josie knew there wasn't a single path that led to all that pain. "I know," Josie added, "but I still have a sweet tooth."

Named Noah. . .

"I think I lost mine." Caroline turned back to the dirty glasses. "I should get back to work."

"Me too." Josie headed for the room overflowing with customers. Every tip took her one step closer to thrusting her debt into the past. And after her shift, she'd try for a taste of the man busting his ass behind the bar.

"You're better than ice cream, pie, and cookies combined," she murmured. "Or at least you were five years ago."

Chapter Eight

BY THREE IN the morning the DJ had packed up and they'd drained the Hoppy Heaven kegs. Noah declared the cows home for the night and the place emptied out. He sent April, the experienced bartender his dad had hired seven or eight years ago to help cover the busy weekend nights, home an hour later.

Josie walked up to the bar. She'd removed her Big Buck's apron. Between her little red sundress and cowboy boots, she looked like the missing "country" in Big Buck's.

"I gave Caroline the keys to my car so she could head home after the dishes stopped piling up," she said.

"You need a ride then?" He lifted the service end of the bar and joined her on the other side.

"And up to Fern's Brewery tomorrow morning. We should take your truck. More space for another keg than in my car."

Noah shook his head and headed for the front door. "Called for a replacement already?"

"As soon as we started running low tonight." She stepped into the parking area while he held the door. "I'm the best assistant manager you've ever had."

"And the only one." He followed her to his pickup. "But, Josie—"

She released the passenger side door, turned, and leaned against his truck. He forgot to say a word about future raises and promotions. His memory hop-skipped back to five years ago. She'd worn a white sundress—shit, he could still picture her outfit—and she'd damn near glowed in the light from the bonfire. And he'd known he wouldn't walk away without tasting her.

Maybe that had made him an ass, a total jerk willing to take what he could get from his friend's wild little sister before he'd left for basic training. He hadn't wanted to go. He'd dreaded leaving his gran and his dad, hell, even the bar. But his family needed a steady paycheck, money sent home to keep Big Buck's afloat. So he'd done the right thing—except when it came to Josie.

And he didn't want to take the high road now. It wasn't like that path had ever taken him anywhere he wanted to go. No, it had paved the way for two tours and made him the enemy in the eyes of the men who should have been like brothers.

He closed the space between them and placed his right hand on the truck beside her head. "Look at me, sweetheart," he murmured.

Her chin lifted and her eyes met his. He swore they

were filled with the same hope he'd witnessed five years ago. He placed a hand on her hip, needing her to stay right here. If she moved away now, they wouldn't find their way back to this place. He'd bury the need and face the fact that he was taking a helluva lot more than he could give.

"Thinking about breaking your rules, Noah?" she whispered.

"You asked for a bonus—"

"Do it, Noah," she murmured.

He lowered his mouth. His lips brushed over hers. One gentle touch before he took what he'd wanted for the past five years.

His tongue swept into her mouth and he pressed closer. She arched beneath, the curve of her ass pressing into the side of his pickup. He ran his hand over her waist, moving higher and higher. Five years and she'd grown softer, her curves more defined, drawing him in . . .

He deepened the kiss as his thumb teased her breast through the layers of clothes. Her hips shifted, pressing closer, and then a leg circled him. The heel of her boot dug into the back of his thigh.

Don't let go. Keep her here.

Right now, here in the parking lot, Josie didn't need him. She wasn't looking for someone to save her, teach her, show her a damn thing. He didn't need to take her for a ride first on an old bull.

She just plain wanted him.

Her hips thrust forward as the muscles in her leg tightened her hold. He stepped one foot forward and allowed his thigh to slip between hers. Balanced, he lifted his hand off the side of the truck and ran his palm over the smooth surface of her thigh. His fingers toyed with edge of her sundress, thrust high on the leg she'd wrapped around him. And then he slipped his hand underneath, searching for more, anything she was willing to give him.

She broke the kiss, panting. "Noah, I need—"

"Anything." He stared down at her. He'd take her right here in the parking lot if she wanted. The cab of his truck. The tailgate. He would stroke her until she came, or kiss her sweet mouth until the sun rose. He'd never ask for more. He just needed to stay right here, with her wanting him.

"You're vibrating," she said, sliding her hand over his chest. A shiver rippled through him, heading lower and leaving him wanting more. When had her fingers slipped beneath his shirt? He'd been so lost, caught up in her. And yeah, he'd tuned out the buzz of his cell phone trembling against his thigh. He'd been a helluva lot more interested in the woman pulsing against him.

He stepped back and withdrew his phone. "Shit."

And that summed up just about everything. The fact that Josie had returned the boot she'd dug into his leg to the ground. The fact that she'd crossed her arms under her breasts as if presenting a physical barrier to further exploration. And the fact that her brother had chosen a pretty damn bad time to call.

He swiped his finger across the screen and lifted the phone. He couldn't ignore the call. Now one of the elite army rangers, Dominic could be freaking anywhere and might not get a chance to phone home again for a long time. "Hey, Dominic."

"Hey, man. Did I catch you while running? You sound out of breath," his friend spoke over the crystal clear signal.

"No, just finishing up for the night."

"Yeah, about that." Dominic's tone shifted, hardening, and Noah braced for the hit. His friend couldn't touch him from half a world away, but he could pack a powerful punch with his words. "My dad said Josie moved back and she's working for you now. How'd that happen?"

He had nothing to give his friend but the truth. "She asked, man. And I had to say yes."

"That's it?" Dominic growled.

"Yeah." Noah looked at Josie. She unfolded her arms and held out her hand.

"Let me talk to him," she said softly.

He nodded, but didn't pull the phone away from his ear. "I got to tell you, your sister is the best thing that's happened to this bar in a while." *And to me.* "She's standing right here. Want to say howdy?"

"It's fucking four thirty in the morning there," Dominic snapped. "What are you still doing—"

"Here she is." He held the phone out to Josie. "Your brother's pissed off."

"WHAT HAPPENED TO SCHOOL? I know you were taking some time off, but I thought you were going back."

Dominic's voice boomed in her ear as she moved away from Noah's truck and into the dark, empty parking lot. Glancing up, she searched for stars or a glimpse of the moon. Nothing but clouds. It was as if the night sky had decided to take a vacation.

But even a dark, gloomy summer's night and her brother's how-did-you-screw-up-this-time tone couldn't penetrate the memory of Noah's mouth crushed against hers. He'd kissed her as if he needed to take her.

"Josie, I know you're still there," her brother said. "I'm on the base in Tennessee. There is nothing wrong with this connection."

"You're coming home?" she asked, torn between wanting to wrap her arms around her brother and keep him safe in Forever, Oregon, and needing a little more time to jump-start her life here.

"No. We're heading out tomorrow," he said gruffly. "To the base in Turkey. Then, we'll see."

"Did you call Dad?" she asked.

"Yeah, which is how I found out you're home and serving drinks at Noah's bar," he said with a sigh. "I thought you were going to finish your degree. You only had one more year."

"I needed more time." *And seventy thousand dollars.* "So I came home."

"That's it? That's why you walked away?" Dominic demanded.

"Life doesn't always work out like you think," she said quietly. *Sometimes it hands you a pile of heartbreak and you need pie. And I think Noah's the perfect combination of sweet and tart.*

But if she said that to her brother, he'd want details.

"No," Dominic said flatly. "It doesn't."

And she wondered if he was thinking about Lily, his high school sweetheart. They'd broken up after he joined the rangers.

"If you're sure about working there—"

"I'm sure," she said firmly.

"Then put me on speaker so I can say goodbye to Noah," he said. "And, Josie? I love you. Don't forget that."

"I love you too," she said softy, hoping it wouldn't be the last time she said those words to him. She walked over to Noah and held out the phone as she found the right button on the screen. "You're on speaker and Noah's here."

"Thanks for looking out for Josie," Dominic said. The hard, threatening edge had returned to his voice, signaling he was done with the I-love-yous. "For treating her like you would your own *sister* and all."

"Dominic," she said. "Don't worry about how he treats me—"

"The hell I won't," her brother snapped. "Do you hear me, Noah?"

"Loud and clear, buddy," Noah said. "I'll take care of her. You focus on doing your job, staying safe, and staying alive."

"Will do," Dominic said. "Will do." And he ended the call.

"Let's go, Josie." Noah took the phone and slid it into his pocket. "Time to get you home before you father sends a patrol car to look for you."

He headed for the passenger's door and she followed. "You're not going to listen to him, are you? He doesn't have the right to jump in—"

"He's your brother. He has every right." Noah opened the door and stepped back, waiting for her to climb into the truck.

She let out an indignant huff, but took her seat.

"The thing is," Noah said, still holding open the door. He was grinning at her, offering a glimpse of his old charm. But the look in his blue eyes was pure sin and stolen kisses. "I don't have a sister. I already warned you, Josie, I'm not some war hero. And I'm sure as hell not a saint."

"No wonder I can't stop wanting you," she murmured. And he laughed.

"Hold that thought for another night," he said. "And whatever you do, don't tell your brother."

Chapter Nine

"YOU HAVEN'T STOPPED by the club." Daphne's voice was lighthearted and upbeat. But even at eight in the morning after too little sleep, Josie could hear the hurt.

Josie sat on the edge of the twin bed she'd slept in until she'd gone away to college. "I've been working every night at Big Buck's."

With this crazy AWOL marine and a boss whom I want to see naked.

"I heard about the Hoppy Heaven," her friend said. "Sounds like he'll keep you around, and for the right reasons."

"I hope so," she said. "I have a payment due at the end of the month."

Reality was like an anchor holding her ship in place and preventing her from sailing straight for happiness. Not that Noah's bed was a beacon of bliss. OK, maybe it was—for a few hours, a single night, maybe two . . . But it wasn't a long-term destination. Not unless she was willing to fall in love with him again and suffer the heartbreak.

Sure, she could push past fear for a night or two. Just like she could march into Oregon's hottest brewery and win a contract. She could reach for a strength she wasn't sure she possessed and play at being bold, even daring. But deep down, she was still terrified she'd stumble head-first into a heartache she couldn't handle.

"So how's Noah?" Daphne asked. "Still surly? Or have you helped him find his smile?"

"He's convinced that he's not the hometown hero any-more," she said. "He claims he's a jerk. And I swear he's trying to prove it."

By pressing me up against the side of his truck.

Silence. Josie couldn't even hear the clink of dishes in the background.

"Daph?" she said. "Did I lose you?"

"You love jerks," Daphne pointed out.

She sighed. "I know."

"He's working tonight?"

"Noah is always working." She stood and headed for the pile of shoes by the closet. She'd dumped her suitcase out, but she hadn't put her shoes away. This wasn't per-manent. She'd come home to get back on her feet. She wasn't giving her shoes a forever home in her childhood closet.

"He's coming by to pick me up soon. We're head-ing to the brewery to pick up another keg," Josie added, plucking her cowgirl boots off the top of the pile. She might as well wear them here. They seemed out of place in downtown Portland. Not that she had a reason to go back. She'd shed her friends, her job, her scholarship, her apartment—every piece of her life in that city had drowned in her depression and mounting dept.

"He might do something nice today and then you won't fall for him," Daphne said, teasing.

"Maybe." But he'd already taken in two women running from pasts that refused to let go. That was sweet of him and she still bought his asshole act. "I suppose there is always the chance we find an old lady who needs help across the street or a kitten who needs to be rescued from a tree," she added.

Daphne laughed, but Josie didn't join in. Because even if Noah saved every lost kitten from here to Portland, she'd still hope for another kiss, another touch, another taste beside his truck.

Maybe I can push my fears aside again and take the risk. . .

"I'll stop by tomorrow morning," Josie said. "I promise."

"Visiting a strip club instead of church on a Sunday?" Daphne said with feigned horror. "What will people say?"

"That I'm still a lost cause. That I haven't changed." She sat on her bed and pulled on her boots that would walk straight back to Noah's barn if she let them. "And they might be right," she added. "Because I want him to be a jerk."

NOAH PARKED HIS truck in front of the chief of police's old farmhouse and pressed the horn. He hoped Josie's dad had already left for the station. Chief Fairmore would start asking questions if he found Noah grinning like a damn fool while waiting for his daughter. And what the hell would he say to Josie's father?

I want your daughter in a way that promises to leave her boots beside my bed—or next to the bull in the barn.

Chief Fairmore might tell him to steer clear of his daughter, or threaten to tell his dad, Big Buck himself, that his son was messing around with an employee. And yeah, Noah probably should have served himself a heaping plateful of regret alongside his eggs this morning. He shouldn't have kissed Josie. But he sure as shit hoped they found their way back to that moment. If she gave him a chance, he'd steal a kiss and then some.

The front door opened and Josie stepped out. She'd skipped the black dress today. And for a split second he missed the tight fit of her red sundress. But then she stepped off the porch and headed for his truck. Between her tight, short jean skirt, boots, and top, his attention splintered, drawn to the legs he wanted to feel wrapped around his hips. And those boots . . .

But his gaze zoned in on her top. She wore the old Big Buck's T-shirt he'd given her that first night. Only she'd tied the loose fabric into a knot at her back, pulling the words "Big Buck's" tight across her chest.

He wanted to replace the worn letters with one word—"Noah's."

He was one helluva jerk. But ever since he'd come home, he'd wanted to lose himself for a little while, forgetting about all the shit that had happened while he served his country.

A blow and a beer—that's what I want.

He'd had a beer, but he'd steered clear of meaningless oral sex with a willing woman. Because he'd wanted Josie since he walked out of that barn five years ago. Smart, sexy, brilliant Josie.

"Morning," she said as she opened the passenger side door to his truck. "You look good for three hours of sleep."

"I've gotten by on a lot less," he said.

"I know." She climbed in and fastened her seat belt. "How is Caroline?"

Still living in a nightmare. But he didn't feel right talking about how he'd heard his houseguest crying through the thin walls in his childhood home.

"All right." He turned onto the two-lane country road leading toward the highway. "She found out about your dad being chief of police."

"I didn't tell her, but I'll make it clear that my father won't find out about her from me," she said. "And I don't think Josh clued her in either. But he did offer to make her a pie."

"What?"

"He likes her," Josie said.

Oh shit.

"If he lays a hand on her," Noah growled, his grip tightening on the steering wheel. "If he touches her—"

"Calm down. You don't need to rush in and save her. Not from Josh Summers," she said. "I have a feeling

Caroline can decide for herself. And one day she might want to say yes to sharing a pie."

"I hope you're right," he murmured. They drove in silence, speeding past one farm after another. Mountains rose in the distance, but they were still firmly in the valley. Cows, goats, and horses dotted the landscape.

"But you're sweet to stand by," she added. "Ready to protect her."

"Yeah? You think your brother is a big old teddy bear for jumping to your defense?" he challenged. *Sweet.* Jesus. He couldn't wear that label, not anymore.

"My brother's not so bad. Especially when he's stationed on the other side of the world. But this isn't about Dominic."

"No?"

"Go ahead," she said, her green eyes sparkling with daring. "Tell me what a jerk you are."

"A damn big one," he muttered.

"I want details." Her low, sultry voice flipped a switch, turning him on.

"Josie, I would strip off a lot more than your panties if we ever found ourselves in a hay wagon. But I'd prefer someplace we wouldn't be discovered." His voice was a low growl and his fingers tapped on the wheel, itching to turn the truck around and take her . . . where?

They couldn't go back to his place. His dad was there. And Caroline. And he wasn't about to seduce the police chief's daughter in her father's house. But Big Buck's?

"Like right here on the side of the road?" she asked. "We haven't passed another car in while. And I don't think the farm animals would breathe a word to anyone. Not that they can see inside the truck."

He glanced over at her, noting the rapid rise and fall of her chest beneath the letters across her breasts. Her T-shirt would go first, out the window. Then, he'd push her skirt up to her waist and draw her panties down her legs.

"Josie, there isn't enough room in the cab of my truck for the things I want to do to you," he murmured, surprising himself by saying the words out loud. He was so caught up in the mental picture of Josie's legs spread and her breasts bared under the sunny Oregon sky. But she'd pressed, asking to see him for who he was now, not the man everyone else wanted him to be, and he didn't want to hold back.

"I'm not asking for anything until I've proven that I have a lot more to offer than a kiss," he added, shifting in his seat. His boxer briefs felt as if they were made of spandex. His dick begged for freedom, eager to greet her in the truck, on the side of the road—anywhere.

She made a tsk-tsk sound. "I thought you had abandoned chivalry. Pull over and we'll draw straws to see who comes first."

He let out a low laugh partly in response to her words, but mostly to keep himself from begging. Sure, sex—oral or otherwise—with a woman he shouldn't touch made him an ass. But there were some lines he refused to cross. He was going down first and he wouldn't take no for an answer.

And that wasn't chivalry. He was being practical. If she wrapped her full lips around him, and if he came in her sweet mouth, hell, he'd probably pass out. The picture racing through his imagination left him damn near dizzy. If she offered the real thing, here, now, she'd have to drive him home.

"Of course, the customers might complain if we don't make it to the brewery to pick up the beer," she added. "But it might be worth the risk."

"Hell yeah." He looked over at her and found her lips parted, her tongue darting out to lick them. She was so damn sexy, so beautiful . . .

He forced his attention back on the road, scanning the shoulder for a safe place to pull over. Wire fencing stretched for miles. The only houses were set back far enough the people inside would need binoculars to know what they were doing on the side of the road. Up ahead the road changed to dirt for a few miles before they hit pavement again. Here was better, less dusty. And he wanted her *now*.

He spotted a road sign up ahead listing the number of miles to the highway and the neighboring towns. He eased off the gas, his gaze fixed on the shoulder and his body taut with anticipation.

Out of the corner of his eye, he saw Josie's arm crossing the console separating the passenger side from the driver's seat. Her fingers brushed his thigh as if urging him on. Like he needed encouragement. He needed to focus and park the damn car before he reached for her. He needed—

"Shit!" He slammed on the brakes and swerved off the road. His desire shut off as if someone had flipped a switch and his training kicked in, driving him to throw the truck into park.

"Noah?"

He heard the alarm in her voice. In his peripheral vision, he saw the hand she'd quickly withdrawn from his leg clutching the seat belt stretched across her chest.

"Stay here," he ordered. "If I give the signal, drive away."

"Wait. Noah, please."

Not a chance. He opened his door. The need to act fact, to eliminate the threat, pulsed through him. He couldn't let anything happen to her. And God only knew what was in the cardboard box at the base of the street sign.

He ran forward and dropped to his knees. His hands hovered over the open box, the realization sinking in that he was in Oregon, not Afghanistan. He couldn't defuse a bomb out here. He wasn't prepared to dismantle a roadside IED.

He blinked and peered into the box for the first time. He felt light-headed and it had nothing to do with Josie's mouth on his dick. The cardboard shifted and a soft mewing sound pulled him firmly back to reality.

"Fucking kittens." He reached inside and picked one up. "Ah, hell."

Dizzy from the rush of relief, he clutched the kitten to his chest and closed his eyes. It wasn't an IED, just some jerk who'd seen a bunch of farms and decided to abandon a litter of kittens on the side of the road for some bleeding-heart farmer to take home to their barn.

He heard the truck door slam, followed by the distinct

click of Josie's boots on pavement. But he didn't open his eyes. She'd been ready and willing to get naked on the side of the road until he'd freaked out.

Because of a box of kittens.

Hero. Jerk. The labels didn't apply. He was a fool. The bundle of fur in his hands sank its sharp teeth into his thumb, and he welcomed the prick of pain, anything to drive away the lingering traces of fear and his own embarrassment.

He opened his eyes and looked up at Josie. She stood to his right with an open field that looked nothing like a war zone to her back.

"You know, this might ruin your I'm-an-ass image," she said, placing her hands on her hips. She offered the shifting meowing box a cursory glance before looking back at him.

"I thought it was . . ." His throat went dry. "I wasn't trying to . . . Jesus, I thought . . ."

I thought the box would explode and steal you away from me. I needed to save you because . . . Because I want you and I'm so damn selfish. . .

"I wasn't trying to be a hero," he added, his voice barely above a whisper.

"Says the man clutching an abandoned kitten," she said.

He set the biting, clawing animal back into the box and met her gaze. He expected to see pity in her green eyes. The poor war hero who mistook a box of kittens for a bomb. But it wasn't there. She looked as if she was waiting for him to get a grip and return to the truck.

If only he could find the strength to get off the ground.

"I could give you a blow job in front of the truck and hope someone drives by and sees us," she said. "That would help cement your bad boy image."

He laughed and this time he searched her face for a sign that she understood. Right now, knees planted in the dirt beside a box of fur balls, he hoped like hell she'd connected the dots. He didn't want to wear the hero label because the things he'd seen, the things he'd done, were flat-out horrible. There was pride in serving his country, and also disgust. Because the people on either side—American, Afghan—weren't divided into bad and good.

And he didn't want pity either. God, he hoped she knew that. Sympathy and sex didn't belong in the same thought. He wanted to hold on to the hope that she couldn't help her attraction to him. Because that would pretty much mirror how he felt. He just wanted to lose himself for a little while—in her.

"So what do you say?" she pushed. "Want a BJ right here, right now?"

"Josie, don't fucking say that if you don't mean it."

Chapter Ten

"WATCH YOUR LANGUAGE in front of my kittens." Josie stared down at the blond warrior kneeling in the grass on the side of the road. He blinked and his brow furrowed. The look in his blue eyes screamed *have you lost your mind?*

"And seriously? You want to?" She nodded to the truck parked a good fifteen feet away from the box he'd expected to explode. "Here? Now?"

"No." He shook his head as he planted one foot on the ground and rose up. "I'm damn near dying to kiss you again. And yeah, I'd like to feel your lips move a helluva lot lower. But not to prove a point to a random passerby."

Thank God. She'd tossed out the offer like a Hail Mary pass at the end of the game. But the goal wasn't to talk him out of his pants. Not here. She wanted to make him laugh and make it clear that she wasn't counting on him for another rescue. If this had been a bomb, she knew he would have done everything he could to save her, but she wasn't about to tell him that. The last thing he needed was her faith in him to carry around like a lead weight he didn't want or need.

"We're taking the kittens," she said, bending down to pick up the box. With the squirming cardboard in her arms, she headed for his truck.

"You're taking them," he corrected, moving to her side and matching her pace.

"Not at my dad's place. He's allergic. But they could live in your barn." She stopped by the passenger side door and waited while he opened it. "I'll stop by and feed them."

He took the box from her while she climbed into the truck. "But—"

"I'm not asking you to feed and play with them," she said. The last thing he needed was another burden. "Just share your mostly empty barn with them for a while. Who doesn't need a barn cat? Or five?"

"Fine." He closed her door and walked around to the driver's side. Once he'd buckled up and turned on the truck, he added, "But you're responsible for the entire litter."

"As long as you don't mind if I stop by your place twice a day." She scooped the smallest of the plain grey cats from the box. The animals meowed, but curled up on her lap once she started petting it. "And maybe if you're nice, I'll take care of you too."

"Nice." He shook his head, but his lips curled into a smile at the sensual suggestion. "Don't count on it, Josie."

"I'm not." And she liked the surly, I'm-not-so-perfect

Noah better. "I might just wait for you to do the 'things you want to do to me' that require more space than the cab of your truck."

"Jesus, Josie," he said as he merged onto the two-lane road. "Let's go pick up the beer."

NOAH NODDED TO the range safety officer and headed for the viewing area of the Willamette Valley Gun Club's range. He'd unloaded five rounds into paper targets, but he still couldn't escape the haunted feeling that had followed him around since he'd spotted the box on the side of the road.

"Noah!" a familiar female voice called.

He glanced over his shoulder and spotted Lena walking beside Georgia Moore. Out of everyone he knew in the Willamette Valley—apart from the World War II vets who camped at the bar in the late afternoons sipping one beer at the pace of a snail—these women would understand the mistake he'd made while driving to Portland. They'd served, though not together, and both returned home with PTSD. Georgia had tried to fight her demons by taking risks. And Lena had hidden away, afraid to let anyone close. Different ways of coping with the same root problem.

But he didn't have PTSD. Sure, he'd had the odd nightmare here and there. But who didn't? He'd seen a box and thought *bomb*. And he'd had to act because, shit, Josie had been in the truck. No, he didn't have residual and reoccurring anxiety from the war. Just a pain-in-the-ass need to keep Josie safe.

"Didn't expect to find you here on Saturday," Georgia said. "I thought your weekends were all work and no play. Or did the kittens change that?"

"April's opening for me today," he said to the petite brunette standing beside Lena. "Wait, how did you hear about the kittens?"

"Katie said her brother Josh stopped by the bar to see your new dishwasher and met the kittens," Georgia explained. "Josh told Chad, who mentioned it to Lena. And Lena told me on the way over here."

Noah stared back the two women. Any other day, he'd welcome the chance to shoot with them. But right now he wished Dominic and Ryan would walk through the door, offer a "hey" and ask what he'd been firing on the range. He wanted to run from the small-town gossip train that now included half the valley. Hell, Georgia lived over an hour from his bar and she knew about the damn cats.

"They're not mine," he said. "Josie rescued them. I'm just keeping them in my barn for a while."

Because I can't seem to stop taking in strays. . .

"Aww," Lena said softly. "That's so—"

"I need to get back to the bar," he said, moving past the ladies to the door. He held an unloaded pistol in his hand, a round of ammunition in the other, and he couldn't escape the mental picture of Josie in his barn, ready and willing to explore all the things he wanted to do to her. He was a lot of things right now, but sweet wasn't one of them.

Noah walked to his truck and stored his gun. He'd come here to feel calm and in control. And he'd walked out on edge. Shooting wasn't going to cut it. Not today. Right or wrong, he needed Josie.

THE BIG BUCK'S parking lot was lined with cars and trucks when Noah pulled up an hour or so later. He'd stopped home to shower, stow his gun, and check on his dad. His grumpy old man had asked a few questions about the bar before settling in front of the television for the night with a glass of whiskey to ease his aching leg.

Noah headed for the back door, waving to Caroline and ignoring the kittens.

"It's crazy in there tonight," Caroline called to him as she loaded a tray of pint glasses into the dishwasher. "Josie said it's a strange mix of locals, mostly guys who've been working on cutting the trees on that big piece of land nearby, the one Josh thought I was trying to protect?"

Noah nodded and paused by the door. He spotted the pie on the counter, untouched, but didn't say a word. He'd talk to Josh another time. Right now, he didn't want to add Caroline's feelings about apple pie to the list of things he needed to fix.

"Josie says the loggers and the frat boys make a wild combination," Caroline added.

"Thanks for the warning." He pushed through the door and headed into the chaos, welcoming the tangible problems a bar full of people who'd been drinking posed.

"Good to see you, boss," April said as he joined her behind the bar. "Can you fill Josie's orders? I'm slammed here."

He nodded and scanned the lines of people demanding drinks. The DJ hadn't even started yet and Big Buck's was packed. Caroline had been right—the juxtaposition of young guys wearing flannel shirts to make a fashion statement and the ones who looked as if they'd spent the better part of the day holding a chainsaw gave the bar a weird vibe. He wasn't expecting a fight to break out. But if they ran out of Hoppy Heaven . . .

"Hey. You're here." Josie rushed up to the service end of the bar. "Show those paper targets who is the boss?"

"Yeah," he said with a smile. "I gave them hell."

"I need three Hoppy Heavens and a shot of tequila," she called as she punched the order into the computer. Her voice was calm despite the chaos around her.

"Coming right up," he said as he reached for a pint glass. After he'd loaded up her tray, he turned to a group of women and took their orders. But he kept an eye on Josie, watching as she doled out drinks. He'd walked in here feeling lost and on edge. The shooting range usually put a cap on the out-of-control feelings. But today? Watching Josie—that was enough. She didn't need him to rush to her rescue. He had a bar full of strays, but no one needed saving tonight.

That's one helluva relief.

Right now, he didn't want to be that guy. He wasn't sure he had it in him to rush to the rescue tonight.

He watched Josie head back to the bar. The sway of her hips drew his gaze to her legs. She wasn't tall, but that didn't change the fact that her legs would feel damn near perfect wrapped around him.

"Stop ogling your employees," Caroline said as she placed a clean rack of pint glasses on the bar for him to put away.

"I wasn't . . ." Shit, he hadn't thought about how this must look to a woman who'd been raped by her superior.

But Caroline laughed softly. "I don't think she minds, Noah. Heck, she looks at you the same way."

The tension eased from his shoulders and he reached for the clean glasses. "I'm not planning to take advantage of her."

"But your assistant manager might take advantage of you," his dishwasher said.

Noah stared out into the crowded bar and spotted Josie. "I hope you're right."

Chapter Eleven

BIG BUCK'S CLOSED at two thirty in the morning that night. Another thirty minutes would have brought in more tips, but the DJ had packed up an hour ago and they'd run out of Hoppy Heaven around midnight.

Josie sat in the back room, sorting singles and fives into neat piles on the metal desk. She'd made enough since she'd started at the bar to send off her next payment to the hospital. Another few shifts and she'd have cash in hand for the doctors. Everyone billed separately. She'd learned that after the burial when the bills had started arriving one after the other in quick succession.

Behind her, Caroline loaded the last of the dirty glasses onto a tray. The dishwasher had tried to drive Josie's Mini back to Noah's place, but the car refused to start. So she'd stayed and kept working.

"Caroline, you can leave the rest of the dishes for tomorrow," Noah said as he pushed into the room. Josie looked up and almost dropped the bills in her hand. Noah was smiling, offering a glimpse of the grin that had come so naturally to him in high school and the years before he'd left for the marines. His black T-shirt might as well have read "I'd look better on the floor" instead of "Big Buck's Bar."

"Josie," he continued as he turned to her.

"Yes?" She'd sampled the worst of what men had to offer—or close to it. (She had a feeling Caroline might win the prize.) But when Noah's blue eyes turned to her, brimming with wanting, the answer was yes. There were some lines she couldn't cross. She couldn't offer her love this time. But the answer to the unspoken need in his blue eyes was still yes. Tonight, her desire trumped her fear.

"Grab your kittens," he said.

Just what every girl wanted to hear. . .

"I'm taking you home too," he added.

"I can't." She glanced at the box of sleeping fur balls. They'd had a bowl of milk earlier, explored the bar's back room and passed out. "My dad—"

"Home to my place," he said. "We'll get the cats settled and then I'll drive you to your dad's."

The three of them piled into the cab of his truck along with the kittens and the pie Josh had dropped off. Josie balanced the sleeping animals on her lap and tried not to think about how Noah had to reach across her bare legs to shift gears. But by the end of the drive, she wanted him to take her from first all the way to third.

"The light's still on," Caroline said. She opened the

door as soon as the car drew to a stop, not bothering to wait for Noah to cut the engine. "I'm going to take my pie up to the house and see if your dad wants a slice."

"He'll grill you for details about tonight," Noah warned. "He'll want to know if we were busy, if we're still a university hot spot."

"Great." Caroline moved away from the truck, leaving the door open for Josie to climb down with her kittens. "I can tell him all about how many dishes I washed."

Noah chuckled. "Hey," he called after Caroline. She glanced over her shoulder. "Mind taking my cell up and plugging it in? I won't be needing it and it's nearly dead."

Um, bullshit.

Josie had seen his phone charging behind the bar all night. Someone didn't want to be disturbed for a few hours—by Dominic or anyone else.

"Sure." Caroline returned to the truck. Balancing the pie in one hand, she held out the other for his phone. Josie passed it over and then watched as Caroline slipped into the darkness, only to reappear on the front steps leading up to Noah's house.

"Come on," Noah said. "Let's get your kittens settled."

Josie followed him out of the truck and across the gravel to the barn. Five years ago, she'd have led the way eager to test the pull drawing her closer and closer to the man who'd labeled himself out of bounds. Back then, Noah had been her superhero, her white knight, and her fantasy rolled into one neat and tidy package. But it had unraveled in the end.

She set the box down by the edge of the cushions

surrounding the bull. What if she crossed the line into naked-kissing territory and it went haywire? Could she handle whatever happened next?

I'd better be able to pick up the pieces. He's made it clear that he's not the guy for the job.

And she didn't want him to play the part this time. She had the money she needed for now. Thanks to Hoppy Heaven, she had some semblance of job security. She was calm and in control of her life. She carried her grief with her, but it wasn't drowning her from sunrise to sunset. She'd been knocked down and she'd gotten back up— with help. She'd buried a baby and she'd moved forward. She could take care of herself and the man who mistook a box of kittens for a bomb. For one night. Beyond that?

Don't think about tomorrow. Focus on the temptation right in front of you. . .

"They're still asleep," she murmured as she stood. She kept her gaze fixed on the plain grey fur balls curled up against each other.

"Good." He spoke from behind her and the sound echoed in the mostly empty barn. "If you won't let me cuss in front of them, you probably don't want them watching this."

His fingers brushed the bare skin above the neckline of her shirt. If she took a step back, she would feel every inch of him, some harder than others hopefully, pressed against her. But she wasn't teasing this time, trying to make her white knight cross the imaginary line he'd drawn around her.

"I've been waiting all day to kiss you," he said.

"Naked kisses?" she asked.

He let out a soft laugh. "Yeah, those too."

His lips touched the nape of her neck and she stepped back. She needed to feel something solid, hold on to someone. His hands wrapped around her hips. He held her inches away from the muscles hidden beneath his clothes. And he kissed her again.

Is there an X on the back of my neck beside my pony-tail? A map of where to kiss me to make me melt? Or do you remember from our bull ride five years ago?

She let out a soft moan as his tongue teased her skin. If there was a map of her body, Noah was the only one who'd bothered to read it. His lips glided across the back of her neck and settled on the other side. He was also the only one who took the time to explore every inch of her.

But she wasn't standing beside his mechanical bull looking to take everything he had to offer—not without offering something in return.

"Ready to prove you're far from perfect?" she murmured.

He released her neck, but tightened his grip on her hips. "Josie—"

"No audience." She pulled free from his hold as she stepped forward and up onto the cushions. "We're not on the side of the road. But you can show me. I want to see how much you've changed. And you can start by taking off your shirt."

He reached for the bottom of his T-shirt and drew it over his head. "I don't know what you're expecting to see."

"You." She studied the wall of pure muscle he'd revealed. His body bordered on physical perfection. Not the bodybuilder physique that left her scrunching up her nose in distaste, but the powerful arms that suggested he could hold her steady anytime, anyplace while he took her. And those abs looked like they were designed to be licked and explored while she headed south.

"Planning to take off your shirt too?" he asked.

She reached behind her and released the knot in her T-shirt. "You don't have any scars," she said as the fabric loosened. She pulled the old Big Buck's shirt off and tossed it aside.

"I was lucky," he said. "Always one truck behind the one that hit the IED or out on patrol when our base was under fire."

"Lucky," she repeated, knowing that bearing witness came with its own scars.

He nodded, his smile replaced by a grim frown. "And you know the crazy thing?" He ran a hand through his short blond hair, leaving it standing up and shooting out in different directions. "There are things I still miss. I liked the challenge and the feeling like I was going out each day and getting something done."

We don't have room for long faces and serious words. Not tonight. Not in here.

"You miss the competition? How about a race? First one to get naked wins?"

Heat and humor chased away the bleak look in his eyes. Yes, this was the man who'd thought about giving her an orgasm on the side of the road, who'd kissed her in the parking lot.

"You're pretty damn set on these naked kisses, aren't you?" he murmured.

She nodded as her fingers toyed with the button on her shorts. "Ready." His hands mirrored hers poised to release his pants. "Set," she continued. "Go!"

She began stripping of her shorts while her gaze remained fixed on him. Her lips parted as he drew down the zipper to his jeans, allowing his pants to sink low on his hips, offering a glimpse of his blue boxer briefs.

He knelt down to untie his boots. She pushed her shorts over her hips and . . .

Oh shit, I should have worn the Converse.

With her cutoff jean shorts around her thighs, she was going to have a hard time getting her cowgirl boots off.

He pulled his shoes off, stood and stripped off his pants. Wearing his boxers and a hard-on she was dying to explore, he placed his hands on his hips. "Not moving too fast there, are you?"

She drew her shorts back up. Should she bend over and pull them off, her bare breasts falling forward? Sitting down and wrestling with her shoes might extinguish the come-and-get-me vibe that she'd tried to cultivate.

"Need a hand?" he asked, his voice a low rumble.

"Yes." She selected option C—lean back against the retired mechanical bull and place her palms flat on the saddle for balance. With her chest thrust out, she lifted one foot and extended her leg to his waiting hands. He pulled her boot off and tossed it aside. Then they repeated the process with the second one.

Her second boot hit the cushion and she released the

bull. She tugged at her shorts. *Stupid, stupid hips.* She glanced down and tried to quickly maneuver out of her clothes.

"I win," he announced.

She looked up and caught him holding his underwear. She heard his boxer briefs hit the cushion, but she didn't look to see where they landed. Maybe the kittens would drag them off and hide them. She certainly didn't want him pulling them back on and covering up seven, maybe eight, long hard and thick inches.

"Wow," she murmured still not looking up from his erection. "You know this doesn't feel like a loss."

"You could claim second place if you stop staring long enough to take off the rest of your clothes. It's not like I have anything you haven't seen before."

Was it her imagination or did he sound a little embarrassed?

"Well . . ."

Five years ago, I didn't stop to stare. I was too caught up in the fantasy.

"How about I help you?" He closed the space between them and reached for her shorts. He guided them over her hips and abandoned them at her feet. Then he returned for her panties. He lowered down on one knee.

"Place your right foot in the stirrup and hold on to that bull," he ordered. "I'm going to take you for the ride I've been dreaming about all day."

You first. But then his fingers wrapped around her ankle and guided her foot into the stirrup and she forgot to protest.

The bottom of her foot brushed the worn leather His hand continued up her leg. He pressed against her inner thigh as his other hand wrapped around her hip, holding her in place. His mouth followed his touch and he trailed kisses higher and higher . . .

"Noah," she gasped as her head fell back. The tip of her ponytail touched the top of the bull's saddle and she closed her eyes.

Again he'd hit the X-marks-the-spot place on her body. He'd offered a naked kiss that promised her first orgasm with a man in more months than she wanted to count. His tongue glided over her as his hand abandoned his hold on her hip and moved between her legs.

"Oh, Noah," she moaned.

His lips and tongue deserted the oh-so-close-to-coming bundle of nerves. "You don't need to use my name over and over, sweetheart. Call on a higher power or just scream."

What the huh? She opened her eyes and looked down at the broad-shoulder blond warrior between her spread legs. Was he trying to avoid recognition for the rioting rush of pleasure rushing through her body, or sidestep the failure on his record if he couldn't deliver?

"I'm giving you full credit for this one, Noah. And I know you won't let me down."

He grinned up at her. "You're that sure of me?"

"Yes."

Please, God, let him finish now.

He teased her entrance, tracing small circles, and then slid two fingers inside. And then he lowered his mouth and flicked his tongue over the place guaranteed to send her free-falling into a world of pleasure.

"Noah!" She screamed his name and the sound of her voice filled the barn. Her hips rocked forward, begging for more from his lips, his tongue, his fingers . . .

Her world narrowed. There was only Noah, the bull at her back holding her steady, and bliss. But the heavens had nothing to do with this fleeting taste of paradise—just the imperfect man at her feet.

"I was right." She managed the words through jagged breaths.

"About?" he asked, drawing his mouth away from her.

"I knew you wouldn't let me down."

Chapter Twelve

Thank God for kittens.

If they hadn't found the box by the side of the road, if she hadn't needed to keep them in his barn, Josie Fairmore wouldn't have led him into the barn and dusted off his pride. He'd been skirting failure ever since he'd deployed. He hadn't stepped in and helped Caroline until it was too late. And shooting at people—doing his job as a marine—it hadn't felt heroic or good. Caroline's rape and the harsh realities of war were beyond his control. His time with the marines had been a wake-up call, forcing him to realize he couldn't always be the guy who rushed in and saved the day.

But tonight, he'd delivered exactly what Josie needed. He hadn't let her down.

And shit, it was a helluva lot more fun to be the guy who delivered the orgasm versus the white knight routine. Who cared if it screwed up his friendship with her brother or messed up their employee/employer relationship? Right now, he didn't give a damn about anything outside this barn, and he was sticking to that story.

"Glad I could be of service," he said as he rose to his feet. His knee felt stiff from pressing into the cushion and his shoulders ached from hunching over to bury his face between her legs. But it beat the side of the road. Although, the scene she'd described, with his back against the front of his truck . . . well, he hoped she planned to do something with the part of his anatomy she'd openly admired earlier. "Now, about your offer from this morning—"

"Yes, Noah," she said with a laugh. She stepped to the side, leaving him facing the bull. "It's your turn to hold on to the saddle while I blow you away. But I don't think you need to wedge your foot in the stirrup."

He followed her instructions, placing his hand behind him on the bull as he faced her. Her gaze flickered to his dick, hard and eager for her lips. But she didn't sink to her knees.

Was she waiting for him to lay her down on the cushion and take her like he had five years ago? He didn't think she was ready for full penetration, "you're mine baby, all mine" sex. He sure as shit wasn't. He was looking for release pure and simple, not a pile of emotions that might spiral out of their control.

And last time . . . the words she'd said while she came, his dick buried deep inside her . . . *I love you*. Yeah, he wasn't too eager to go there again.

"Sorry." She gave her head a little shake. "I didn't look long enough last time. I didn't fully appreciate your cock.

I knew you were bigger and better than anything I'd ever seen, but I only caught a glimpse or two."

He grinned because right now, with her, he sure felt like smiling his damn ass off. "I don't think I got enough of your dirty talking mouth last time."

She laughed and dropped to her knees. Her hands touched his thighs and, thank you Jesus, her lips wrapped around his dick. Her tongue swirled around the tip and she took another inch, and then another . . .

"I'm feeling pretty damn appreciated," he growled as he released the saddle and ran his fingers into her hair. He pressed against the dark locks pulled tight by her ponytail and hoped she wouldn't feel the need to respond.

She took him deeper and he closed his eyes. The rest of the world faded into a distant noise. The sound of Josie sucking on him, drawing him deeper, trumped everything else. The feel of her nails digging into his thighs, the bite of pain in sharp contrast to the nearly overwhelming I'm-going-to-explode feeling coming from his dick.

Her head bobbed faster and faster. Yeah, he was close, too far gone to hold back.

"Josie," he cried as his hips thrust forward, driving him deeper into her mouth. A warning bell sounded in the back of his head. *Not like this. You have to warn her if you're going to come in her mouth.*

"I'm going to . . . Oh God, Josie." He pushed her head back and released her. Wrapping one hand around himself, he ran his fingers to the tip, once, twice, and he came. All over her breasts.

He looked down, expecting to see confusion, maybe a

hint of hurt in her eyes. But she was focused on his hand. And miracle of miracles she was smiling as if she'd secretly hoped he'd explode on her chest.

She shifted her green eyes upward to meet his gaze. "Quite the gentleman, aren't you?"

He laughed and lowered down to his knees. He released his dick and reached for her, wrapping his hands around her shoulders. "Josephine Fairmore, we're in a barn and you're a mess. That doesn't make me much of a gentleman."

She pulled away and crawled on her hands and knees over to his discarded shirt. She picked it up and wiped her chest. "There. All clean. And bonus, you'll have to drive me home topless."

"Stay." He said the word without pausing to think through the repercussions. He couldn't take her to the house where his father was eating pie with Caroline. And keeping the police chief's daughter overnight? That probably spelled trouble, like serving a shot of whiskey to a drunk.

"Here?" she asked, patting the cushion. "With the kittens and the bull?"

"Here."

Because it damn sure feels like trouble can't touch us in here.

And because he wanted to hold on to the feeling that he could give her what she needed for a little while, that he wouldn't fail her.

"OK." She crawled over to him, her nipples close to

brushing the mat. He wanted to taste her, draw her breath into his mouth, but he needed to hold her more.

He lay down on his side and patted the mat. She joined him and he wrapped his arms around her, pulling her back close to his front.

"Noah?"

"Yeah?" He ran his hand over the curve of her hips before settling on her waist.

"This sure feels like chivalry to me," she teased. "Offering to cuddle instead of driving me home after a BJ in the barn? You could have dropped me off, headed home and passed out alone with a beer in your hand."

A blow and a beer. He'd come home thinking that was all he wanted. But right now, Josie topped that list.

"Sweetheart, I don't even have a blanket," he murmured. "Though I wouldn't mind the beer and the passing-out part."

He closed his eyes. The realization that he was pushing close to exhaustion surfaced and he gave in, content to drift off to sleep with Josie in his arms.

And not a chance in hell her brother will interrupt this time.

"Noah," she whispered.

But he was too close to sleep to respond.

"I don't need a blanket," she added. "Just this."

NOAH WOKE UP to the feel of a woman's breast cupped in his left hand, her head resting against his shoulder, and a trio of kittens curled up on his chest. Yeah, this came close to heaven in his book. And it didn't have anything to do with the plain grey balls of fur purring like they had little motors. Or the repeated knocking at the door.

He lifted his head off the cushion, trying not to disturb Josie. One of the kittens yawned and stretched as his abs contracted, but he ignored the animal. He focused on the tap, tap, tap against the bar door. It was real, all right.

How the hell did Dominic get back here so damn fast?

Daylight streamed into the barn through the windows in the rafters. It was morning and he was bare-ass naked beside the bull with Josie Fairmore.

If someone catches us, this will be a helluva lot worse than when she was caught in the hay wagon with Travis holding her panties.

"Noah?" Caroline's voice called through the door. "Noah, are you in there?"

"Yeah," he called back before she tried to open the barn door. Had he locked it last night? He'd been focused on Josie. The rest was a damn blur. "I'll be right there."

He gently slid his arm out from under Josie. Then he set the kittens on the cushion and stood. He found his pants and pulled them on, ready to go commando if it kept Caroline out of the barn.

"You're leaving?"

He looked back and saw Josie propped up on an elbow, blinking away the sleep. The band tying her hair back had fallen out during the night, leaving her long dark wavy hair flowing over her shoulders. A few strands fell forward and teased her breast. He wanted to join her on the matt and keep the rest of the world locked outside the barn while running his tongue over her nipples.

"Noah," Caroline called again. "It's important."

His jaw tightened and he looked away from Josie. "I need to talk to her and find out what's happened," he said softly.

"Noah, wait."

He glanced back. She was alert and sitting up now, her legs crossed. She plucked her hair band off the mat and began pulling her hair back.

So damn beautiful.

"I should go," he said, the sight of her breasts draining the conviction from his voice. But if Caroline said it was important . . .

Caroline didn't ask for help. Even when she'd been afraid their commanding officer would attack her again on the way to the bathroom, she'd never reached out to him. He'd offered because he saw what was happening and he couldn't live with himself if he didn't try to keep her safe.

Caroline wasn't asking now, but still, she'd searched him out. And she was smart enough to guess he hadn't spent the night in the barn to keep the kittens company.

"I should see what Caroline needs," he added.

"I don't have a car." She lowered her arms, leaving her hair in a messy pile on her head.

"Take my truck." He reached into his pocket and withdrew his keys. "Just leave it at the bar if you get your car running, OK? I'll find a way to get there."

He tossed the keys and she caught them. "Thanks," she said. "I'll see you at work later."

He nodded, knowing he should say something more. *You blew my mind last night. I never wanted it to end. I still want you.*

But he just turned and headed for the door. The woman on the other side needed him. And Josie? Shit, she'd been the one saving him last night. Maybe later he'd find the words to tell her.

Chapter Thirteen

JOSIE'S MINI SPUTTERED to a stop in front of The Lost Kitten. She'd had to jump her car off Noah's truck and she had a sinking feeling her little red car would die again when she turned it off. Stupid battery. But it had made it to her friend's club. Thank goodness. She'd thought about taking Noah's truck out to see Daphne.

"Not after the way he ran out of the barn the minute someone came knocking," she muttered, then turned the key and listened as the engine died.

And the way my heart raced to the door just in time to see it slam shut.

She'd taken the risk and tried to fight her fears. And she'd ended up falling for him all over again. If only he hadn't asked her to stay the night.

She climbed out of the car and walked through the empty parking lot. Daphne stood in the door to the special events room she rented out for bachelor and bachelorette parties. She'd even hosted a baby shower there once or twice. Daphne had offered to throw one for Josie. But she'd been dead set against telling anyone in Forever about the baby. And then it had been too late.

Stupid reality raising its ugly head, stealing away the feeling that everything was all right. . .

"Morning," Daphne called. Wearing a pink T-shirt that read "Naughty Kitten" across the chest and jean shorts, her best friend held a mug in one hand and a vibrator in the other.

"You sure know how to greet company," Josie said.

Daphne shrugged. "I figured you needed one or the other. Coffee if you jumped Noah or an orgasm to remind you why you should."

She took the coffee and pushed past her friend into the party room. Or what had been the party room the last time she'd been inside. Maybe it still was—for a very different kind of party. Lingerie that would be better described as costumes—no one wore a French maid's outfit on a night when they planned to enjoy a cup of tea and a book—handcuffs, and a laundry list of things Josie couldn't identify lined one wall. Unopened boxes filled the other side of the room. "What happened in here?"

"I'm redecorating," Daphne explained.

Josie sipped her coffee. "I think you're going to lose the baby shower market."

"The event space wasn't bringing in enough, so I'm turning this room into an adult toy store. I'm calling it The Lost Kitten's Toy Chest."

"A sex toy store?" Josie said. "Just outside Forever?"

It was a bold move. But unlike Josie, Daphne Sullivan had never been concerned with her reputation. Her father had walked out when Daphne was three, leaving her mother, a church secretary at the time, to raise Daphne and one-year old twin boys alone. With three children to feed, Mrs. Sullivan had decided men spent more on sinning than redemption. She'd used her meager savings to open The Lost Kitten. While God might have forgiven Mrs. Sullivan, the churchgoing women in Forever hadn't extended an olive branch—to either her mother or Daphne. Her mother probably didn't care, given that she'd moved to Washington to care for one of the twins' children. And the whips on the walls suggested her daughter didn't either.

"The town needs one." Daphne set the vibrator down on a box and reached for a folding chair propped up against the wall. "Sit, drink your coffee, and tell me everything while I unpack boxes."

Josie explained about the kittens, the ones that didn't belong anywhere near her friend's toy chest. She left out the part about Noah mistaking the box for a bomb—and what they'd done during their night in the barn. Daphne didn't need to know the details. How Josie had been grateful he'd told her to place her foot in the stirrup, how she'd needed the stability when his tongue gave her the orgasm to end all orgasms. And maybe that was a tiny exaggeration. If it really was an orgasm for the record books, she'd still be so lost in pleasure that she wouldn't care about how he'd run away with her heart this morning, would she?

Daphne dropped a bottle of body paint on the floor. "Wait, he left you naked in a barn because the new dishwasher needed him?"

"She's an old friend," Josie said. Telling this story was like weaving her way through a maze. She kept running into roadblocks, things she didn't feel comfortable revealing to Daphne—like the fact that Caroline would be arrested if anyone found out she'd run away from her duty to serve with men who'd threatened her.

"Noah's right, you know." Daphne bent over to pick up the paint. "He's a jerk."

"I know." Josie stared into her coffee cup. "And now I need to tell that jerk, who happens to be my boss, that I can't go back to his barn."

"You're falling for him," Daphne said.

She nodded. Last night, she'd slipped a few inches closer to love.

"Shit, Josie." Her friend's brow furrowed with concern. "I'm sorry."

"I landed myself here. Just like every other mess. But this time there's nothing pulling him away. He doesn't have to leave for basic training in a few hours. He's not heading to war."

"That might not be such a bad thing," Daphne said. "If you're falling in love—"

"I'm not ready to get my heart broken again," she said flatly. "So this time, I'll have to push him away."

Please let me be strong enough.

"You can do it." Daphne reached for another box.

"After everything you've conquered? Telling that jerk to fuck off won't be a problem."

"As long as I don't mix up the words. One look at him, Daph, and I might say 'fuck me.'" She stood and scanned the unpacked boxes. "I'd stay and help, but I really need a shower and maybe a nap before my next shift. Next time?"

Daphne nodded. "I'll save the edible underwear section for you." She picked the vibrator up off a closed box. "But you should take this. To help you keep your hands off a man who thinks it is appropriate to leave you alone in a barn wearing your birthday suit."

"Caroline knocked on the door—"

"Stop defending him."

"He had to leave." Plus, they were lucky the dishwasher had stayed outside. And that her gun was in the safe. Not that the AWOL marine had a reason to shoot. But if something had pushed Caroline to seek Noah out, she was probably feeling closer to her GI Jane–meets–wood-nymph persona than her recently adapted position as Big Buck's freckle-faced dishwasher.

"When you told me that you planned to ask him for a job at Big Buck's I thought he might be good for you." Daphne plucked a plain brown paper bag off her desk and slipped the sex toy inside. "That he would help you move on from all that pain."

"I am moving on," Josie said, hoping her voice hadn't wavered. She could tell herself she was strong enough to move forward, to put the past behind, just a few more bills to pay and she could shed the guilt, bury the pain—but that didn't mean it was true.

"I visited you in the hospital, remember?" Daphne had softened her tone. "And afterward? When you refused to leave your apartment?"

She nodded. No one else, aside from the food-delivery men, had witnessed her hopelessness. She'd avoided her father's calls. Dropped out of school and cut ties with her college friends. She'd isolated herself from the rest of the world.

"I know you're fixated on paying your bills—"

"I have to do something," Josie said.

Daphne held out the bag with the vibrator. "Call me tomorrow."

"You want a status report?" she said, eyeing the bag.

"I just want to know you're OK."

Josie took the bag. "Me too, Daphne. Me too."

NOAH STARED AT the image on his phone. He knew that parking lot. The picture showed the small rear space behind Big Buck's. Hell, even his truck was in the shot along with Caroline and Josie. The words covering the image read "Mine." And whoever had posted this wasn't talking about the truck.

"This appeared on my phone this morning?" he asked, looking up at Caroline.

"I was in the kitchen making coffee when your phone vibrated. I glanced at the screen, more out of habit than anything else, and saw this picture."

She stepped back and began to pace the small kitchen. The half-eaten apple pie sat on the rectangular wooden table. The table ate up half the room, but his dad had turned the formal dining room into a home office after his mother passed away.

"And you think Dustin sent this?" He leaned back in his chair.

"Who else would hunt me down? Who would know to look for me here? He knows where you work. You talked about the bar all the time." She stopped and shook her head. "I shouldn't have stayed. I should have warned you and left, taking him with me."

Noah sighed. "He sent it to my phone. Whoever sent this, he's not just after you."

And he could be after Josie.

His grip tightened on the phone. He didn't like the idea of someone hunting down Caroline. But Josie? Goddammit, he wanted to reach through the phone and crush whoever had sent this.

"I know. Dustin's after you too. " She started to pace again. "We're an easy target if we stay together. I should leave."

"And go where?" he asked. "I like the odds of two against one crazy, bitter, and disgraced marine."

"You believe me? You really think he's coming for us?"

"Yes." He'd always taken her at her word.

"Thank you," Caroline said. "For believing me."

"You don't exaggerate or look for drama. Until all that shit started when we deployed to that remote FOB, you did your job."

Sure, she'd endured off-color jokes during basic and possibly during her first deployment. He hadn't been stationed with her on that one. But when they arrived at the forward operating base in Bumblefuck, Afghanistan, some members of their team, led by Dustin, had changed. Maybe something snapped when they went out searching for the enemy and returned knowing they'd taken lives. Or maybe they'd simply parked their decency and restraint at home.

"He's coming for us. For you." Caroline let out a shrill laugh. "I'm nothing to him. You're the one who provided the evidence that stripped him of his rank and destroyed his career."

"I know."

This wasn't a box full of kittens. This was a viable threat. And it was hitting close to home, not far from the barn where he'd slept with Josie last night. He'd been lost in the feeling that he'd finally found someone who wanted what he had to give. And the entire time, a pissed-off ex-soldier, who was probably armed and undoubtedly dangerous, had been lurking around his hometown.

Shit, he hadn't offered Josie a rescue last night. He'd brought her too damn close to the kind of trouble that led to bullets flying—or worse. Now, he needed to keep her safe. And Caroline too.

"Do you have a plan?" she demanded, her gaze moving between him and the screen in his hand. "Should I start packing?"

He set the phone on the table. "You don't need to keep running from him."

"Dustin might alert the police," she said, but he swore her spine straightened and she stood taller. Caroline had always preferred fight instead of flight.

"We'll deal with that if it happens." He stood. "But if he's waited this long, I don't think he plans to hand you over to be court-martialed. I'm guessing he realizes that you'll be parked behind a desk instead of thrown in a military prison as punishment for deserting."

"This is personal for him," she acknowledged.

"Right."

"Unlock the gun safe. We'll go after him now."

It was tempting. But after seeing Caroline aim at Josie, his faith in her only ran so far. Caroline had been hurt by people she'd trusted to have her back when bullets were flying. That betrayal had left her on edge. When they were still deployed together, she'd grown more and more paranoid.

"I doubt he's still in the parking lot waiting for us after sending this," he said. "But you can have your gun back if you promise to only use it for self-defense."

"You have my word."

His cell vibrated in his pocket. He withdrew it and glanced at the screen. Two words stared back at him—*Josephine Fairmore*.

"Shit." He swiped his thumb across the screen and held it to his ear. "Hey, Josie."

"I need you to pick me up."

"What happened? Where are you?" he barked into the phone as he pushed back from the table. His fear for her rushed to the surface.

"The Lost Kitten parking lot. And my car won't start. Daphne jumped it, but this time it has finally called it quits. I think it needs a new starter."

Relief washed over him. *Thank you, Jesus, for keeping her safe.* And yeah that was the closest he'd come to praying in a while.

"Which stinks," Josie continued. "Because even if I did the labor myself, I can't afford the part."

"We'll figure something out," he said. "Just stay there. I'll borrow my dad's Buick and swing by to pick you up."

"Thanks. Daphne would give me a ride, but she's opening soon for brunch."

Sunday brunch with strippers. He didn't want to think about who headed straight for The Lost Kitten after services.

"I'll be right there." He glanced at Caroline, who'd assumed a parade rest position with her hand clasped behind her back. She'd been ready to launch into action in response to the panic in his tone when Josie had said she needed him.

"And then, Josie," he added, looking away from Caroline, "we need to talk."

Chapter Fourteen

JOSIE KICKED THE front passenger side tire of her broken-down Mini. If her stupid car had waited until she arrived home to break down, she wouldn't be waiting for a blue Buick that looked like it belonged in a museum to pull into The Lost Kitten parking lot and save her.

It wasn't entirely the car's fault. She could have driven Noah's truck over here, flat out ignoring the fact that it felt wrong. They weren't a couple. She worked for him. And after last night, that's where she drew the line. Or she could have cancelled on Daphne. But this morning she'd needed a friend. After facing so much alone, it was a relief to have someone who knew her past and her present waiting just across the town line. And she couldn't have possibly known in grade school that she was picking a best friend who gave away a silicone penis over coffee.

She folded the brown paper bag closed over the tip of the vibrator as the Buick turned into the parking lot.

I should have called my dad and begged him to send a deputy. Or waited for Daphne to take a break and drive me home. But too late now.

Plus, she wanted to put their "talk" behind them. And then they could both focus on work. She had a hunch he wanted to deliver the same message she'd been searching for the strength to deliver.

Last night was great but. . .

"Thanks for driving out to get me," she said as she slid into the passenger seat and fastened her seat belt. "I would have waited for Daphne to give me a ride, but right now I can't tell what I need more—a shower or a sandwich." Her stomach rumbled, driving home her point.

"Daphne didn't offer you food?" he asked, nodding to the bag.

"Or a shower, even though I probably have hay or something from your barn floor in my hair."

Go ahead. Launch into your talk. Please say the words first.

"We haven't kept hay in the barn for years," he said, guiding the old car through the turn. "So what's in the bag if it's not food?"

She studied his profile. He looked just as blond, scruffy, and serious as the day she'd first asked him for a job. Nothing like the man who'd insisted on holding her close last night *after* he came on her breasts.

"A gift from Daphne." She reached into the bag and withdrew the vibrator. Noah glanced over. His eyes widened, and his brow furrowed.

"What the . . . ?"

He turned his attention back to the road and made the turn onto Main Street too fast and too sharp. The fake penis fell out of her hands and onto the floor.

"Daphne had some strong feelings about the way you left this morning," she said as she reached forward to pick it up.

"I'm guessing she's not the only one." He stole a quick glance at her. "This is only about this morning?"

"No one is insulting your skills. Trust me, you've made better use out of that mechanical bull than probably every rodeo-riding cowboy in the West. And I'm guessing your equipment is better too."

"Jesus, Josie—"

"Though contrary to what half this town believes, I don't have a lot of basis for comparison," she added.

"I'm sorry about this morning," he said.

And this is the point where I tell you I'm sorry too, but I can't go back to the barn with you.

"If you put that thing away, we can grab a table at The Three Sisters while I explain everything."

"You're buying?" she asked, silently cursing herself for not saying the words and pushing him away.

"Yeah."

She reached for the vibrator at her feet and shoved the toy back into the bag. She didn't want it. But Noah?

I'm making a mess of things. I should tell him to drive me straight home. I can't do this.

"What did Caroline need?" she asked, as if that tidbit of information was her reason for following Noah into the café.

"I'll tell you while we eat," he said grimly.

He docked the Buick in a parking space a half block from the café and the alley where he'd rushed to her rescue five years ago. This man and his hero routine. If only it didn't speak to her heart.

She followed him into The Three Sisters Café. She didn't say a word until they'd settled into a corner table set for two with brightly colored cloth napkins and mismatched silverware. Nothing in The Three Sisters matched. When they'd first opened, before Josie was born, the now ancient triplets had traveled from garage sale to yard sale to anywhere that sold cheap tables, chairs, and silverware. They'd gathered the items and opened a restaurant. Some of the pieces had price tags fixed on them and could be purchased after your meal—if you wanted an old chair that never had a hope of being mistaken for an antique.

Noah rested his arms and started talking. He paused when the waitress appeared to take their order, but otherwise offered a detailed explanation of why Caroline had come knocking on the door. She'd listened while he explained about the photograph. She could connect the dots too. He didn't need to spell it out. The man who'd raped Caroline had followed her to Oregon. They couldn't prove it—not without going to the police and exposing Caroline's unauthorized absence—but their former leader was baiting them.

"Josie, I'm to blame."

And judging from the pained expression on his face, he believed those words.

"You're not responsible for a madman's actions," she

said. Part of her was still surprised their we-need-to-talk conversation didn't involve the words "last night can't happen again" or "it's not you, it's me." Although, she still planned to deliver the line "it's not you *or* me, it's us barreling toward heartbreak."

"But I brought him into your life," Noah said flatly.

"Yes, but I'm the one who demanded a job at your bar," she said. "And I plan to keep it."

He nodded. "I can't make any promises. Not anymore. But I'll do my best to keep you safe. It will be easier if you're working at Big Buck's."

"He's not after me, Noah."

"Maybe not, but once he realizes you're . . . that we're . . . connected"—Noah leaned back and ran his hands through his hair—"I don't know what he'll do."

"About our connection." She twirled her fork in circles on the table. "Last night was great, but . . ."

"You'd rather have the toy Daphne gave you," he said.

Yes. No. Maybe? A vibrator wouldn't send her spiraling into feelings she couldn't handle.

"I need to focus on paying my bills, Noah. I can't afford—"

"Josie Fairmore," Elvira called, following the waitress carrying their breakfast over to their table. "I didn't see you in church with your father this morning."

"I wasn't there." She accepted her plate, but didn't bother offering Elvira a smile or further explanation.

Elvira nodded to Noah as she took his plate from the young server. But she didn't set it down on the table. "This boy is working you too hard."

"I'm just grateful to have a job," Josie said as she picked up a piece of bacon and stared at the *man* across the table.

"I always thought you'd do better after going away to school." Elvira still held Noah's plate as if still debating whether to serve him.

Josie looked up at the woman who won the award for the nosiest of the triplets. "You're probably not the only one in this town."

"May I have my breakfast?" he asked.

"True," the old woman said, ignoring Noah. "But I never thought it was your fault that you lost your undergarments to Travis Taylor. That boy couldn't manage to lead his team to the state championship. Not like Noah here." She finally set the plate down in front of him.

"Noah doesn't like to talk about it," Josie said firmly. "Not football or his time with the marines."

NOAH STARED ACROSS the table. Ever since Caroline had shown him the picture, he'd been trying to figure out how the hell he'd keep Josie from getting stuck in the crossfire when Dustin attacked. If there was one thing in his life he wanted under his control it was Josie's safety. He refused to fail her.

But she'd turned the tables on him, jumping to his rescue over breakfast.

"Humph," Elvira muttered, glancing at Noah and then back at Josie. "Enjoy your breakfast." And then the nosy triplet walked away before asking if they needed anything to go with their bacon, eggs, and hash browns.

"Now about last night," Josie said, careful to keep her voice low.

Ketchup. He wanted a bottle of Heinz and an escape from this conversation. And hell, while he was asking for things, he wanted Josie in his bed putting her new toy through its paces. Then he'd toss it aside and—

"There's something about you," she continued. "You kiss me and I feel myself falling for you."

No, Josie. I'm not the guy you fall in love with, not then and not now.

"But I'm not ready. After everything . . . I need more time to put my life back together."

"Yeah, the timing's off," he said. *And I'm not sure I should be trusted with your love.*

He'd just watched her rescue him from another pat on the back for his football days when he should have been the one jumping in. He should have told Elvira to shove it when she brought up church and Josie's panties.

But I want you.

Looking at her across the table, remembering how she looked last night pressed up against the bull . . . part of him didn't want to let the moment turn into another memory he carried with him for five freaking long years.

"But, Josie, the timing might always be off."

"It might," she admitted. "But—"

"Relax and eat your eggs. I'm not asking for a demonstration of your new toy. Not on a Sunday."

She picked up her fork. "You are a jerk."

"I know." She could call him anything she liked as long as she stayed safe.

He dropped his gaze to his plate. Somehow, he had to make that happen. He couldn't fail Josie. He couldn't rush to her rescue after the fact. Not like he did with Caroline. No, this time he had to have the upper hand from the beginning. No one would hurt Josie Fairmore again. That was one promise he planned to keep.

But none of that changed the fact that he wanted to see Josie test her vibrator.

Yeah, he was one helluva jerk.

Chapter Fifteen

THERE WAS A mad marine on the loose, probably armed and sure as hell dangerous, and all Noah could think about was the sex toy in Josie's locker. But she was running scared from him instead of straight into his bed.

He shoveled ice into a pint glass with a ferocity that left the barely legal coed on the other side of the bar wide-eyed.

"I can have a beer if a Bloody Mary is too much trouble," the young woman said.

"No trouble." He forced a smile and reached for the tomato juice mix he kept on hand for Sunday afternoons. The university crowd confused four in the afternoon with brunch time. "Plus we're out of the Hoppy Heaven," he added.

"I love that beer," she said and launched into a monologue about how she used to drive to Portland with her girlfriends to pick up four-packs for their respective boy-friends.

"Here." Noah thrust the Bloody Mary across the bar, cutting off the story. "I'll start a tab for you."

The door to the back room swung open and he turned away from the chatty customer. Josh Summers emerged wearing jeans and a button-down shirt that fit the description of dressed-up logger.

Noah raised an eyebrow as the youngest Summers brother approached the bar. "When did you start using the back entrance?"

"Thought I'd avoid the crowds," Josh said with a smile and a shrug.

"I have five paying customers, counting the vets drinking pop and swapping war stories at the end of the bar."

Josh held up his hands in mock surrender. "You caught me. I was delivering a pie to your dishwasher."

"She gave the last one to my dad," he said, knowing "shared" might be a better description.

"Generous. I like that." Josh claimed a stool in front of Noah and leaned forward, his forearms pressing against the wood. "You know she's carrying, right?"

"Yeah." He'd unlocked Caroline's gun from the safe that morning. "Do you want something to drink?"

"Beer. Whatever you recommend. I don't need the fancy stuff."

Noah nodded and turned to pour a pint.

"She told me that she has MST," Josh said as Noah

turned around and handed him the glass. "Military sexual trauma, right?"

Noah nodded, unsure what to say. He didn't think Caroline talked about what had happened. Hell, she'd never used the official term with him.

"I'm guessing that's why she went AWOL and someone's after her now?" Josh continued.

"It is," Noah said. "And why you might want to reconsider your plans to bake a third pie."

Josh looked down at his beer and shook his head. "It figures that when I decide I'm ready to settle down, to find what my brothers have, I'd fall for the one woman who's a long way from having so much as a conversation alone in a room with me."

"And if she's arrested, Caroline might face time in a military jail," Noah added.

"That would be a new spin on long-distance."

What the...

Noah rested his hands on the bar and leaned forward. "You're planning to ask her out?"

"No," Josh said. "Right now, I want to be her friend. I know what it's like to work your way back from something you're not sure you can overcome. And hell, I've seen Lena struggle with her post-traumatic stress."

"This is different," Noah cut in.

"Of course it is." Josh met his gaze across the bar, his smile gone. "But I look at her and I see a beautiful, determined woman. I'm not going to walk away because it's hard to be her friend right now, and impossible to hope for more. Everyone has their problems, man. It's all about how they face them. Caroline did whatever it took to find you and warn you about whatever has her carrying a handgun while washing dirty pint glasses. I have to admire that."

Noah nodded as the door to the back swung open a second time and Josie marched into the room. She'd faced a helluva lot and yet here she was, smiling at customers. She'd buried her child and still refused to give up on paying his bills. Guilt and pain had hit her hard. But she was fighting back. Dammit, he loved that about her.

Love?

A decent dose of "fuck me" settled on his shoulders, threatening to force him to the ground with his head between his legs so that he didn't hyperventilate. But he fought back. Of course he loved Josie. She was like family. One night in a barn—shit, make that two nights now— didn't lead to falling in love. Not that he was prepared to tackle that particular challenge right now, piled up onto everything else.

But maybe love didn't have to be a challenge.

And he sure as shit shouldn't use it as a reason to walk away from Josie, even if she was pushing him to the door. They'd been friends for too long. He wasn't about to give that up. Plus, he knew she was safe when she was serving up drinks in his bar.

"Plus, I like Caroline's girl-next-door freckles," Josh continued, drawing Noah's attention back to the man sipping his beer across the bar. "They're cute. Not what you'd expect from a woman who enlisted in the marines."

"She's tough," Noah said, knowing her "cute" looks had attracted their CO too. He'd heard the guys talking about them.

"Yeah, I get that. She pulled her gun on me when I came in carrying a bourbon pecan pie."

"She's on edge." He should probably reconsider letting her have her weapon. Although he doubted that he stood a chance of getting it back now.

"Sounds like she has every reason to be. Then she smiled and put it away when she saw me. You know, I think she liked my pie. Even if she did give it to your dad."

"She might," he admitted, still watched Josie out of the corner of his eye. She laughed with the girl sipping on her Bloody Mary.

I should ask her if Caroline's pulled a gun on anyone else. I should find out if her dad plans to drop by, and make sure he uses the front entrance. I should tell her that I admire her. That I want her. That I know she's afraid of getting hurt. Shit, I'm scared I'll be the one to hurt her. But dammit, I want to help her face her fears...

He slapped his palm on the bar, silencing the voice in his head. "Hold on a sec." Then he turned and walked to the service side of the bar. "Josie," he called.

She glanced over her shoulder, then headed his way. The sway of her hips beneath her fitted black skirt drew his attention south. She'd paired the black mini with a pair of beat-up Converse sneakers and the Big Buck's Country Bar T-shirt he'd given her the first night. Her hair was still damp from her shower and pulled into a librarian's bun at the back of her head. She was an oddball mix of comfort and sexy as hell. She stopped on the other side of the wood access panel to the back of the bar.

He leaned forward and dropped his voice. "How about a dinner break when the rest of the staff arrives to man the bar? It's quiet today."

Her brow furrowed. "Noah—"

"If we pick something up to go, we could swing by the barn and check on the kittens. You're responsible for feeding them, remember?"

"I'm not going to forget about my kittens—"

"Josephine," a deep male voice called.

Aww hell. Noah closed his eyes. He'd know the chief of police's voice anywhere.

He blinked his eyes open and glanced over his shoulder. Josie's dad was off duty, judging from his jeans and worn flannel shirt. But Noah was still relieved he'd used the front door—even if it cost him a dinner break in the barn with the man's daughter.

"JOSEPHINE."

The deep, male voice carried through the bar. She could count on one hand the number of people who used her full name, and they were both immediate family. She turned and spotted her father. She'd bumped into him earlier, when she'd stopped home to shower. He'd been busy watching golf, and looking like he was headed for a well-deserved nap on his day off.

"Hi, Dad." She met him halfway to the bar, before he moved closer to the door leading to the back room and the dishwasher determined to aim first and ask questions later.

"Stop in for a drink?" she asked, tearing the handwritten list of orders off her pad.

"Not tonight. I came to see you."

"Oh?" Her hand clutched the torn slip of paper.

"Does your boss give you a dinner break?" He nodded toward Noah, who had turned away to pour a beer behind the bar but remained within earshot.

Only on the days when he wants to visit the barn.

"You bet, Chief Fairmore," Noah called as he turned off the tap. He delivered the beer and returned to the middle of her bar, not far from her dad. "We're slow tonight, and I know you don't get much time off from keeping our town safe, so take your time. Enjoy dinner."

"Thanks." But her father moved closer to the bar instead of the door. She followed and slipped the drinks orders across the polished wooden surface to Noah, who glanced at them briefly before looking up at her dad.

"Have you heard from Dominic?" her father asked.

"He called the other night," Noah said, but his expression didn't offer a hint of emotion.

"While he was stateside?" Her father spoke as if he were conducting an interrogation.

Did someone see us kissing in the parking lot and report back to my dad?

But then how would they know Dominic had called? And why would her father care about the fact that she'd messed around with her brother's friend, now her boss?

She wasn't a teenager anymore. Plus, she made it clear she was a lost cause when it came to finding trouble.

"Yes," Noah said.

"Oh." One word and Forever's tough-as-nails police chief deflated like a balloon stabbed with a pin.

"Dad?" she said tentatively. A dreadful feeling simmered and threatened to shake the calm she'd struggled to maintain since Noah had left her in the barn. If something had happened to Dominic . . .

Her father shook his head. "He usually calls on Sunday mornings. I knew he was heading out this week. He never says where. Syria. Afghanistan. Africa. He's been all over the world. But he always gives me a heads-up if he won't be able to call."

Noah frowned. "I'll shoot him a message while you're out. I doubt he'll respond, but I can try. If you're worried, I can email Ryan too."

Josie's hope rose. Ryan was the third member of their trio from high school and the years following. Of course, he'd keep tabs on Dominic too.

"I hadn't thought of that," her dad said. "How's he doing? I haven't run into his father in a while."

"Ryan's making the most of what the air force has to offer. And with their budget, that's a helluva lot. I swear he joined just to play with their toys." Noah reached for a pint glass to fill the order she'd passed to him. "Different branches and all, but Ryan talks shop with Dominic."

Her father smiled, but it appeared strained. "I'm sure the air force has a lot of toys, but not much beats the army rangers."

Navy SEALs. They probably had one up on the rangers. But she wasn't about to stomp on her dad's pride. His son was a ranger. He'd completed a training program most guys failed. She couldn't recall the exact pass/fail rate, but she bet her dad knew. And he'd probably told the entire police force.

"Let's go, Dad. Before the dinner hour is up," she said, hoping she could keep his mind off Dominic for a little while. Her brother would be fine. He had to be OK. If he wasn't . . . how much loss could one person take?

Chapter Sixteen

"I HEAR YOU'RE a local hero."

Josie dropped her breadstick and looked up at her dad. Hero? Her? She glanced around the mostly empty mediocre Italian restaurant, the only establishment aside from The Three Sisters that didn't cater to the university students.

"For bringing in that special beer?" her father added, his brow furrowed as if he was trying to focus on small talk instead of thinking about Dominic.

She let out a laugh. "That's right. I'm the local beer hero."

"Glad you're putting that marketing degree to good use," he said, reaching for his water.

"I didn't finish my degree, Dad."

The waitress arrived and took their orders. Josie took her time ordering a house salad and personal pizza, hoping her father would drop the subject of school.

"You could always go back," her dad said as the waitress walked away.

"I could," she admitted. *But first I have to pay seventy thousand dollars in medical expenses I never told you about. . .*

"Or take classes at the community college to finish up your degree. That way you could live at home."

"And you could keep an eye on me?" she said, reaching for her water.

The town's chief of police offered a rare smile. "I like having you home, Josie. You still haven't told me why you came back, but I'm glad you did."

"Me too, Dad."

"And I wouldn't mind some help with the mowing," her dad added gruffly. "Maybe you could do some work in the old vegetable garden. It hasn't been weeded much since you ran off to college."

But Dominic was the gardener.

No, she couldn't say his name. Not right now.

"I can try, Dad. But if the tomatoes go on strike like they did the last time you put me in charge, well, remember you asked for my 'help.'"

Her father leaned his head back and laughed. "I'll tackle the tomatoes if you handle the beans. I never liked them much anyway."

She smiled as the waitress set down their salads. "Deal."

Maybe she could salvage this relationship. After everything she'd been through, maybe she could find a place here, at home.

BY MIDNIGHT, DINNER with her father felt like a distant memory. Big Buck's didn't have a DJ on Sunday nights, but the place had filled up with patrons hoping for a pint of Hoppy Heaven. Josie had served up a tray full of disappointment all night long. The tips were dismal.

The local beer hero, my ass.

She set two bottles of light beer in front of the dudes in the corner booth and walked away before they could complain about the empty keg. She didn't want to hear about how she'd let them down when it came to their drink of choice. She stomped back to the bar to pick up the next round.

Who wanted to claim the "beer hero" title anyway? It didn't have the same ring as Noah's claim to fame. "Football star" or "veteran warrior"—those labels deserved respect. Noah had done something brave, something to be proud of—he'd served.

But apart from the deal with the brewery, what had she accomplished? She'd survived the loss of a child she wasn't supposed to have in the first place. She'd lived through asshole boyfriends and grief.

No, it was better to stick with her Hoppy Heaven claim to local fame. Everything else she'd "accomplished" stemmed from bad decisions.

Joining the army, the marines—those were solid, good choices.

Selfless.

Brave.

Although it hadn't exactly worked out that way for Caroline. She'd survived her own assholes and grief.

At least the jerks from my past haven't driven me to carry a gun.

Josie stopped in the middle of the crowded bar. People moved around her, talking and drinking. Was that the upside here? She'd come so far, pulling herself out of a grief that threatened to eat her alive, and the only bright side was that she didn't have to carry a weapon?

"The cows are home for the night, folks," Noah announced, his voice cutting through the crowd.

"Hey, what about last call?" one of the dudes in the booth called.

"Finish up what you have and head out," Noah said, his gaze landing on Josie. "We're done for the night."

She lowered her chin and focused on her worn Converse sneakers. He was jumping to her rescue. Had he caught the college kids staring at her as if she'd broken their hearts by not having their favorite beer available tonight? Or had he heard from Dominic? Maybe Ryan had responded with bad news?

Her head swam with what-ifs and she headed for the bar.

"What's wrong with your cows?" another man called. "It's not even one in the morning."

"On a Sunday," Noah muttered. But then he raised his voice and called out, "Sorry. The dishwasher is broken."

Caroline. He's rushing to her rescue tonight.

"Oh, Noah," she murmured, her voice too low to be heard over the grumbling customers. "You can't save everyone."

Just like she couldn't keep stumbling into heartbreak and then putting herself back together.

One day I'll just be broken.

No, she needed to steer clear of another night in the barn with Noah. Even if it meant begging him to feed and water the kittens for her. And she should probably leave her new toy in her locker. She didn't even want to risk closing her eyes and dreaming about him while alone in her bedroom with a silicone penis.

"Josie, I'm going to run Caroline home," he said as he slipped out from behind the bar. He paused and glanced back at her. "Are you OK to stay and help close up? I'll come back for you after I drop her off."

She nodded and met him by the door to the back room. Keeping her voice low, she whispered, "Did something happen?"

"Our dishwasher aimed at a raccoon by the Dumpster when she took the trash out," he said wearily. "She's on edge and armed. I need to get her out of here before she does something stupid." He ran his hand through his short blond hair. "And hell, maybe I should start paying her not to clean the dishes or set foot anywhere near the bar."

"But then how would you keep an eye on both of us?" She hoped to make him laugh, or even smile. But he just shook his head and put on his doom-and-gloom expression.

"I don't know, Josie," he said. "I don't know."

"NOAH, BEFORE I get in your truck, I think you should know . . ." Josie paused midspeech and drew a deep breath. She stood with one hand on the open truck door and the other on her hip. The bar was at her back, dark and locked up for the night.

What now?

What more could he possibly add to his middle-of-the-night to-do list? He needed to send another message to Dominic because the first one hadn't led to an A-OK response, and Chief Fairmore had looked pretty damn worried. Then he planned to search the woods around his childhood home for his former commanding officer. And shit, someone needed to feed and water the fucking kittens. All that before falling dead asleep for a few hours, getting up and opening the damn bar again.

"I left the vibrator in my locker," she said, her tone practically daring him to demand that she march back into Big Buck's and get it. Because tonight was the perfect night to say "screw you" to the people he needed to help and focus on sexual fantasies and orgasms.

He eyed Josie. Beauty and determination were one hell of a turn-on. It might not be such a bad idea. After all, who was he to play the hero?

"Josephine Fairmore, get in the damn car. I'm not leaving you alone in a parking lot beside your broken-down car just because you don't want to share your toys. I was planning to take you back to your dad's place anyway."

Because I really need to get started on my list.

"Turning in early?" she challenged in a voice that said *I wasn't born yesterday.* She climbed into the truck and secured her seat belt.

"No." He pulled out of the parking lot and headed for

the main road while he filled her in on his plans for the remaining hours before sunrise.

"You're really worried about Dominic?" she asked softly when he'd finished.

"I think your brother can take care of himself. But I don't like seeing your father worried. And right now, I can't have Forever's chief of police dropping into the bar and asking questions. If Caroline had pulled the trigger on that raccoon, if everyone in the bar heard a gunshot tonight? The police would be everywhere. And she'd be headed for a jail cell."

They rode in silence for a few minutes, passing through Forever's dark and quiet downtown.

"Did you take away her gun again?" she asked.

"Yes." He accelerated as they reached the town limits. "I hadn't realized how close to the edge she was. But the stress has done a number on her. She's more likely to get herself hurt, hit an innocent bystander, or even you. And I can't let that happen."

"I'm glad you took away her gun," Josie said slowly as he turned down her driveway.

He fought the urge to press on the gas and fly over the gravel to her house, kick her out of the truck, and speed away. If he didn't get her out of here soon, he might reach for her.

"And I appreciate your desire to keep me safe," she added. "But I can take care of myself, Noah. I've been doing it for the past five years."

He put the truck in park in front of her house and turned to her. She'd said those words as if she was still trying to convince herself. And he knew a helluva lot about that.

"You're wrong, Josie. If I don't take care of you, who the hell is going to look out for me? Who is going to bring me back to reality when I see a box and think it's a bomb?"

Her eyes widened and she lifted her hand to his cheek. Her palm brushed against his stubble. Shaving hadn't come close to making his to-do list.

"Noah—"

"Last night, you took me away from all the bullshit," he said, looking straight into her green eyes. "You gave me a break from wondering how the hell I'm going to keep from letting people down when they need me. How I'm going to maintain control . . ."

"But I don't need you," she said softly.

"Are you sure about that?" He lifted his hands and cupped the sides of her face. Yeah, she was running scared. But he didn't want to let her go. "Because I think we could take care of each other."

"Noah, what are you asking for?" she demanded.

"You," he said firmly.

He leaned across the center console and pressed his lips to hers. He fought his way in, kissing her deeply, needing her to feel how much he wanted to escape into that place where he could fulfill her desires—no doubts, no questions.

Her fingers pressed into his cheek and her other hand touched his thigh. *Higher. More. Don't let go.*

He groaned. His tongue touched hers, his lips took

more. Her fingers dug into the muscles as her palm ran higher and higher on his leg.

This wasn't the time or the place. Hell, her father was inside. They weren't kids, or anywhere close to it. But still—

She broke the kiss, drawing back and taking her hand off his thigh. But she didn't release his cheek.

"Noah." She said his name as if it was important that he was the man in the truck kissing her. But when he stared into her eyes he saw the hint of panic. "You can't have me. I'm not . . . That's not what I'm . . . I came home to find a job. Yes, you look even better than you did five years ago. And yes, I asked you to break the rules. But I'm not ready. After last night . . ." She drew her lower lip into her mouth, her brow furrowed, then added, "I just can't. Not yet."

Everyone had problems. Josh was right about that. And Noah wanted to take on Josie's. Not the bills and the need for cash. Those were tangible and could be fixed over time. But the loss and the heartbreak? The feeling that she had to face the world alone without turning to anyone? He wanted to shoulder those problems.

Because then maybe she'd take on his.

"Just don't push me away," he said. "I can be your friend."

Her eyes narrowed and she released her hold on his cheek. "Just friends? No naked bull rides?"

"No naked anything if that's what you want," he said.

She folded her arms across her chest and gave him a look that called bullshit. "Just friends who rush in and save each other? Who wait for the carrier pigeon to deliver a cry for help?"

He nodded. "I want you in my life, Josie. Because I'm waking up to the fact that it sucks to face the world alone."

JOSIE STARED AT Noah, her fingers reaching for the door. The teasing, the flirting, the little game they were playing, pretending they could fool around without heading for something serious—it was all over.

"I think it's easier," she said, "if fewer people know about your troubles. There's less judgment that way. Plus, going it alone has worked for me."

"Some people help." His gazed darted to her hand and then back to her face. "Without judging."

"You don't understand," she ground out. "What you did? Going to war? People feel bad about themselves if they judge you. But me? I wasn't supposed to have a baby. How am I expected to make them see him as a person? Morgan was just over a pound, and I only got to hold him once, but he was my little boy."

"Josie, you're not to blame for what happened," he said.

"Whose fault is it then?" she shot back, releasing her grip on the door and turning to face him. "The doctors and nurses did everything they could."

"It's not yours," he insisted.

His hands wrapped around her shoulders, his grip solid and firm as if he'd never let her go. He pulled her close into a hug. And tears threatened. With his arms around her, his lips pressed against her ear, murmuring comforting reassurances . . . oh dammit, she'd proven his point. She wanted this. Him. If only . . .

She pushed away. "It is my fault. I'm to blame. I didn't carry my baby long enough. There must have been something I could have done differently, something I missed. A couple more weeks, months even, and he would have been fine." She opened the door and moved to climb down.

Her grief, her loss—that was all on her. And she had to pay the price. Her shoes hit the gravel and she released the door. But even with the heartache, she wouldn't change a thing. She'd held Morgan once and it had been worth a lot more than seventy thousand dollars. Now she just needed to focus on paying what she owed and not losing her heart again.

"Josie, don't go. Not like this."

"I've been living with this for over a year," she said softly, glancing back at him. The light in the truck illuminated his pained expression. "I don't need a rescue from grief. Go home, Noah. Help Caroline. Search the woods. Feed the kittens. They need you."

"And you don't," he said.

"No." She plucked her handbag off the front seat floor and stepped away from the truck. "Goodnight, Noah."

"Night, Josie."

She closed the door, but stopped an inch before she closed him out. "You'll remember to check on the kittens right?"

"I'm not that much of a jerk," he said with a half-hearted smile.

She stepped back. She waited for the truck to pull away, but it remained still, engine rumbling, on her gravel drive. Shaking her head, she turned and headed for the front door. She had moved past sneaking into her dad's house. But she knew Noah wouldn't leave until she was inside, safe and sound.

"You're not a jerk," she murmured once the door was closed and locked behind her. She headed for the front hall window to watch as he pulled away. "Not at all."

And that was part of the problem. There was a point when she'd wanted to lose herself in the kiss. His mouth had claimed hers and it would have been so easy to let him possess her.

But she had a scar—invisible maybe, still she felt it— from the last time Noah had walked away. Not as big as the one left by Travis, though she knew it was thanks to sheer luck and Noah that her high school sweetheart hadn't left a visible mark. Or as painful as the reminders of Morgan's father, the man who'd left her pregnant. Still, she wouldn't let Noah Tager carve out another piece of her heart.

"Josephine?" her father's voice called from the den. She heard the whisper of sportscasters in the background.

"I'm home, Dad."

She turned and walked into the room. Her father was in his recliner, remote in hand, watching a baseball game.

"Did Noah drop you off?"

"Yes." She sat on the couch that had been the dogs' favorite perch throughout her high school years. "My car needs some work."

"I could lend you a hand sometime."

She forced a smile. "That'd be great. Thanks. I think it's the starter. Stupid Mini. I bought it used in Portland. Easier to park in the city."

Her dad nodded slowly and turned to her. "So did Noah hear from your brother?"

The hope in his voice nearly brought her to tears. Had her father spent the last five years moving around this big, old farmhouse, watching his dogs pass away and worrying about her brother? Alone?

I needed you, Dad. I was alone too and scared to ask for help.

She reached over and placed her hand over her father's rough, aged skin.

"No, Dad," she said softly. "Not yet."

Chapter Seventeen

"IF YOU WANT to keep working at the bar, I need to lock up your gun." Noah pushed away his empty pie plate and stared across the kitchen table at his dishwasher. He couldn't have her waving a weapon around in the back room. Next time she might accidentally shoot Josh and then they wouldn't get another pie. And the youngest Summers brother knew how to bake.

"But Dustin's close," she said firmly. "What if he shows up at the bar? Or the house? You saw the picture. He could be out there right now." She waved to the window.

"Caroline." He reached across the table and covered her hand with his. Her slice of breakfast pie remained untouched on her plate. "I walked every inch of this property and half the neighbor's last night. We only have ten acres. If he'd been out there, I would have seen him."

"He sent the text not long after I found your barn,"

she protested, withdrawing her hand from his hold. "He's following me."

"He's not out there now. I'm not saying he won't turn up. But when he does I don't think it will be good for anyone if you have a gun. You scared the hell out of that raccoon last night and you didn't even fire."

She folded her arms across her chest. "I heard the noise and I was so scared."

He sat back in his chair. "Not everything is an attack. Not around here. You're safe, Caroline. I'm going to make sure no one turns you in and I'm going to protect you from Dustin. You'll just have to trust me."

She nodded and withdrew the gun from the waistband of her pants. "I do. I know you'll do your best to keep me safe and hidden. I'd feel better if I could help . . . but you're right. It's not just Dustin. Every noise feels like an attack is imminent."

He took the pistol and removed the bullets. At least one of the women he was trying to keep out of reach of a madman wanted his help.

"But I'm keeping the job," she said.

"That's fine, Caroline. I'm going to take a shower and then sleep for a few hours before heading into work."

He pushed back from the table, feeling the ache in his muscles from hiking until past dawn this morning. At some point, he needed a full night's sleep. Maybe a return to the first few days back when he'd taken over the bar from his dad. He'd crashed after closing and slept until midmorning. Some days he'd gone for a run before opening the bar, but most of the time he'd fit in a little physical training or a trip to the gun club when April showed up. Simple, easy days. And there had been no chance to play the hero.

The floorboards creaked and groaned as he climbed to the second story. He headed for his bedroom, pulling off his T-shirt as he walked. The walls were pale blue and covered in pictures from high school. There was a blank space above his wooden headboard where he'd once hung a "The Few. The Proud. The Marines." poster. He'd ripped it down when he'd first walked into the room after returning home.

He scanned the other walls as he removed his boots and jeans. Dominic stared back at him from almost every shot. And Ryan was in most of them too.

"Dom, I need you to come home and kick my ass for laying a hand on your sister," he murmured to the picture on the bedside table. He stood in the center holding up a trophy. "I need something to keep me away from her."

Because it feels a helluva lot like she is the only one I want and need.

He stripped off his pants, tossed them on the unmade bed, and headed for the attached bath. Running his hand over his chin, he turned to the mirror. He should probably shave too, but he was too damn tired.

Where the hell had Dustin disappeared to? He turned on the shower and stepped under the cool stream without waiting for the water to warm. He hadn't seen any signs of a campsite, or even footprints in the wet ground from the light rain a few nights back.

He suspected their former CO was trying to terrorize

Caroline. Back on the base in Afghanistan, the scumbag had laughed when he'd run into Noah escorting Caroline to the bathroom in the middle of the night. He teased her for needing a chaperone to take a piss. It had taken a helluva lot of restraint to keep from punching the higher-ranking marine. But Noah had held back knowing Caroline deserved her day in court.

And all the bastard got was a slap on the wrist for adultery. I should have knocked him out when I had the chance.

This time, he would land a hit or two. While he'd taken Caroline's gun, he planned to keep one locked in his truck.

"Noah!" He heard a pounding on his bedroom door as Caroline called out a second time. "Noah!"

"In the shower," he said, doubting she heard him over the water. He leaned his head back, rinsing the shampoo out.

"There's a . . ."

He couldn't make out the rest. He turned the water off, stepped out, and reached for a towel.

"Did you hear me?" The panic was rising in her voice and she screamed through the door. "There's a patrol car out front!"

Noah secured the towel at his waist and headed for the door, leaving a trail of water on the linoleum bathroom floor and then the carpeted bedroom.

"Did an officer get out of the car?" he demanded, opening the door.

A pale-faced Caroline shook her head.

"Might be Josie's dad," he reassured her. Without

bothering to take the time to pull on clothes, he headed for the stairs. If they were here for Caroline, if someone had tipped them off, he couldn't let her meet them alone.

He reached the kitchen and spotted the car sitting in the gravel parking area that separated the house from the barn. The side read "Forever Police Department." And he breathed a sigh of relief. Not the state troopers. He knew every cop working under Josie's dad. Hell, maybe his neighbor had reported him for snooping around his property by the chicken coop at dawn.

But the door to the police car didn't open. Noah pushed through the door to his house and scanned the front seat of the car. The person in the driver's seat had long, dark hair.

Josie?

"What the hell?" With the faded blue towel keeping his private parts out of view, he walked out onto the porch. "Stay here," he called to Caroline.

"Shoes would have been a good idea," he muttered as he crossed the gravel to the car. He headed for the driver's side window and knocked.

Josie turned to look up at him. Her fingers maintained a white-knuckled grip on the steering wheel. And her eyes . . . red and overflowing with tears. Her cheeks were wet. Even though her hands maintained a tight hold on the wheel, her arms trembled as sobs shook her body.

"Josie!" He pulled opened the driver's side door and took a knee right there in the gravel. He didn't care if the rocks tore his skin to pieces because one look at her face, a mask of pain and anguish covering her go-to defiant expression, and he knew. Someone had died.

Dominic.

He reached up and placed his hand on her cheek. He didn't trust himself to pull her from the car. Even kneeling on the ground, his legs felt like Jell-O. As soon as she said the words—the ones that he fucking knew were coming—then he would need to turn away from the truck and throw up.

Gently, he turned her face toward his. "What is it, Josie?" he whispered.

"Dad got a call early this morning." She hiccuped as the tears trickled faster and faster, rushing over her cheeks and his hand. "Dominic was injured."

"Injured. Not dead?"

She nodded and he placed his free hand on her leg to keep from falling forward with relief.

"Not dead," she said, her voice still trembling. "But it's bad. They didn't provide details. I don't know how it happened, where he's hurt, or where he was. Just that they're moving him to Germany and he'll need surgery."

Noah squeezed her thigh. "He's strong. Your brother will make it through surgery."

"But the thought of him in a hospital alone." She closed her eyes. "I've counted on him being the best, the strongest, the smartest ever since he left. He *wanted* to serve. And I trusted him to always be the one out of the two of us who would succeed. He's the star. I know he's fighting, going to dangerous places, but I always thought he'd be all right."

"He's not dead yet," Noah said. But he knew that thought wasn't high on the comfort meter.

"I know." She opened her eyes and looked at him. "I also know all about sitting and waiting for it to happen."

Ah hell.

"You're not alone this time," he said, his voice rough with emotion. "And, sweetheart, you can't give up on Dominic. He's going to pull through."

I need him to make it out of surgery and get his ass back here.

"I hope so," she said, her words hollow. And yeah, he'd bet there was a fifty-fifty chance she believed them.

"Where's your dad?" he asked. "He must be upset." Wasn't that a fucking understatement? This might break the police chief.

"My dad left for the airport. He packed a bag and climbed into the truck after we got the call. I don't think he stopped to book a flight. He just planned to show up at the terminal and find a way to get to Germany. He left his patrol car behind. I was supposed to take it to the station, but I came here first."

Suddenly aware of the gravel digging into his knee, and the fact that he was wearing a towel, which wasn't covering much with him kneeling like this, he released her face and withdrew his hand from her leg. But before he could stand, she reached for him and grabbed ahold of his wrist.

"I'm not ready for this, Noah. I'm not tough enough to see my dad cry, or, or any of it." She glanced around the sedan. "Right now, I don't even think I could drive this car back to the station. It's a miracle I made it here."

"You should go to Germany," he said, the words out before he'd thought them through. He wanted her here, with him. But she'd be safe in Germany. And she'd be with Dominic just in case Noah's faith in his friend's ability to pull through didn't hold.

She let out a harsh, dry laugh. "I can't afford it."

"If the army hasn't offered to cover your travel and lodging that's a good sign," Noah said. Part of him wanted to quiz her on every little detail from the early-morning call. But he didn't want to scare her.

"They did." She blinked as if trying to fight a fresh wave of tears. But her efforts were no match for her grief. "But I'll miss work. And I have bills due."

"Go. I'll cover your lost wages and tips." With his free hand, he gently removed her grip on his wrist. Then he leaned into the patrol car and drew her out. He slipped one arm under her legs, his other supporting her back.

"Noah, it's too much," she murmured.

"I'm not worried about the money, Josie."

But I'm fucking terrified for you, and for Dominic.

"If you're sure."

Slowly he straightened, cradling her in his arms. "Please, Josie. Just say thank you and let me help you this time."

He was aware of her face pressed against his chest. He'd dried from the shower, but now her tears dampened the hair. Even though she was crying, she felt so damn good in his arms. Someone to hold on to. Someone to keep him from falling apart.

"Thank you," she murmured. "But you don't have to carry me."

Holding you tight? That's for me, sweetheart. To keep me from falling to pieces in my driveway while wrapped in a towel.

He tightened his hold and headed for the house. "Let me take you inside, get you a piece of pie, and then we'll book your ticket. Later, I'll find a way to get the patrol car back to the station. I'm sure your dad's deputies understand. He's probably briefed them by now."

He kept his voice low and soothing as he rambled. If he were in her shoes—and shit, he was pretty damn close, Dominic had been like family to him—he'd want a barrage of reassurances blocking the bleak what-ifs from parading through his imagination. What if Dominic had already lost too much blood? Or what if his friend had lost a limb? What if he stayed alive but was never the same?

Noah clenched his teeth as he reached the porch steps. He refused to cry. Not here. Not now. He'd give her pie first. Get her settled. She didn't need to see him fall apart.

"The pie's pretty good. It's the one Josh dropped off for Caroline." He pushed through the door and headed for the kitchen table. Scanning the room, he didn't see Caroline. He had a hunch she'd disappeared. Whether she'd run out of fear or out of respect for the emotional moment they'd shared in the driveway, he wasn't sure.

Kicking the chair out with one foot, he lowered her down. And his blue bath towel followed her feet to the kitchen floor.

"I need to get dressed." He'd retrieved the only thing

keeping his naked ass covered while he focused on being a friend to Josie. She'd come to him. After last night, when she'd made it clear she didn't need anyone, she'd driven straight to him. And he was pretty damn sure it was because she needed a friend.

He secured the towel around his waist and headed for the door. "Pie is there on the table. Plates are in the cupboard to the right of the sink and forks below. Help yourself."

He took the stairs two at a time, half listening for movement in the kitchen. It sounded like she'd found the plates. Now, he needed clothes. And then . . .

He stepped into his bedroom. Dominic's face stared back at him. There was a whole fucking collage from their senior year. He spotted Lily curled up in friend's lap. Lily and Dominic side by side after a game. Someone had called Lily, right? Dominic had broken up with her. First after he'd left for basic training and then again when he'd completed Ranger School. Noah had taken it as a sign that Dominic didn't plan to call Forever home again. He guessed Lily had too. But she still stopped by the bar now and then to ask about him.

Pulling off his towel, he hung it over the pictures. He turned around and there was Dominic's face again. The three friends in their uniforms, arms slung across each other's shoulders. He kicked the table and the frame fell forward, crashing into the wooden surface.

What the hell happened out there, Dom?

He thumped his fist against the wall over the nightstand. But fuck—hitting the wall hurt. Leaning his head forward, he closed his eyes and let the tears flow. He'd fought to hold them back since he'd run to Josie's side in the parking lot. But now he felt like he was going to explode if he held them in any longer.

"Don't you fucking die, buddy," he murmured, his face still buried against his arm. *"Please."*

"Noah?"

He lifted his head, but didn't turn to look at her. He didn't want to give her proof that she'd walked in on him naked, crying, and hoping like hell her brother would live.

"Yeah," he said gruffly.

"I heard the banging." Her voice grew closer with each word. He felt her hand on his back, gently resting on his shoulder blade. "I wanted to make sure you were all right."

He glanced over his shoulder. *Fuck it. Let her see the tears.* She'd come here red-eyed and weeping. She hadn't tried to hide her pain.

"I'm not, Josie. I'm so damn far from OK." He turned around, letting her see all of him, broken down and battered by the news that his friend might die and there was nothing he could do about it.

"Me neither." She reached her hands up and cupped his cheeks, wiping away his tears with her thumbs.

He reached for her, pulling her close, needing to feel her cheek against his chest, her body against his. And yeah, he was still naked. He should probably ask her to wait outside while he found some damn shorts, and then take her back to the kitchen for more pie.

"Noah?" she whispered.

He closed his eyes and rested his chin on top of her head. "I'm scared," he murmured.

"That he'll die?" she asked, her voice trembling.

That he'll die. That if he makes it, he won't even recognize himself.

He felt her tears start to flow as if he'd turned on a faucet. Shit, he was a jerk for making her cry again.

"Josie." He lifted his head, placed his hands on her shoulders and drew her back. Her eyes swam with helplessness and fear. And he wanted to make it all go away. He wanted to erase her pain and strip away his own. He hated the fear, demanding his attention.

But what the hell could he do?

His gaze fell to her parted, trembling lips. He could escape. The fear, the pain, the tears . . .

He lowered his lips to hers. Running his tongue over her lower lip, he waited for her to push free.

But her arms wound around his neck. Her fully clothed body pressed up against him. And he kissed her harder, deeper, losing himself in the feel of her mouth. She tasted like sugar and bourbon. She was intoxicating.

And right now?

She was saving him.

Chapter Eighteen

JOSIE UNDERSTOOD GRIEF. She could navigate the fog that descended when the Bad News Bears arrived and delivered their doom-and-gloom message.

Your brother has been injured.

Your brother needs surgery.

She had heard those words and the haze had swallowed her. There was no way out. She knew that. The bears stood guard, keeping her locked in fear and anguish.

Until Noah kissed her.

One kiss from a man who was fighting the same fears didn't change a thing. But oh God, it felt so good. The touch of his lips, the feel of his hands pulling at her shirt as if he needed to touch the skin beneath . . .

Her body responded, demanding more, needing to feel more. She ran her hands over the smooth skin of his broad back, down to his waist and around to his chiseled abs. Her tongue touched his as she traced her fingers over his six-pack.

So much strength.

Gliding her hands upward, she pressed her palms flat against his chest, dimly aware of his fingers toying with the button on her pants. He tugged at her zipper, but didn't bother pushing her pants down over her hips. He simply slipped his hands inside and drew her to him, keeping a firm hold on her ass.

Groaning, she broke away from his kiss and tipped her head back. His mouth trailed kisses over her jaw, down her throat, as if he needed to taste every inch of her.

More. I need more.

She wanted to keep the fog of grief locked outside his bedroom. She didn't want to think. She just wanted to feel. She needed him right now because she couldn't step into that place where the world felt like it was falling apart, spiraling out of control. Not yet.

"It's not fair," she murmured, her eyes open and staring at the ceiling.

His lips hovered over the swell of her breasts peeking out over the top of her shirt. "Not much is."

Oh no, don't go there.

"You're naked and I'm not," she said, drawing him back to this place where physical desire dominated.

He let out a low laugh as his tongue glided over her skin, licking just above the edge of her T-shirt. "Not fair at all."

She broke away from him and stripped off her clothes. Her movements were rushed and she nearly fell over trying to get out of her pants. But she wasn't looking to seduce him. She wanted to take him, fighting her way to a mutual pleasure that would block out everything else.

His brow knitted together as he watched her. "Are you sure—"

"Shhh." She placed her index finger over her lips. "I need you, Noah. I'm not calling, sending a letter, or a pigeon. I'm right here and I need—"

His lips captured hers, his hands on her hips, drawing her close and then guiding her back. Her legs touched the bed and she lowered down, sitting on the edge. She took him with her.

I won't let go.

Noah dropped to one knee, his hands moving to her breasts. She leaned back and he followed, moving over her.

Wrapping her legs around his hips, she held him close. He didn't pull away, or try to second-guess her. He just slid inside.

"More," she whispered.

He stared down at her, his cheeks still damp from his tears. But he wasn't crying now; he was looking at her as if she was everything he needed. And he was pumping into her hard and fast. There was nothing gentle or care-ful about his movements. It was as if he needed to take as much as he could, as if he was depending on her . . .

I can't be strong enough for both of us.

She closed her eyes and let her hands roam. He had to meet her halfway, rescue her just a little . . .

His hips slammed into her. His right elbow pressed into the bed beside her shoulder and his upper body hovered over her. But his other hand wandered, gliding over her torso, reaching between them. His thumb brushed over the spot guaranteed to send her spiraling into pleasure. But then he stopped.

She opened her eyes and looked up at him. *I promise I won't turn into an idiot, calling out professions of love.*

"Ready?" he demanded. "Because I can't hold back."

"Yes," she gasped.

He thrust into her again, his thumb offering one more teasing touch as plain old missionary pushed her over the edge. She took the sweet relief, holding tight to the pleasure. She did not love this man. She refused to hand over her heart.

But she loved everything about this orgasm.

"Noah. Oh, Noah." She chanted his name as if it would prolong the escape.

But one more thrust and he groaned, his face contorting as he came. His lips curled back and he looked as if was growling, a pure animalistic reaction to taking her, claiming her, and oh God—

"We didn't . . ." she said, her hand pushing at his chest, trying to get him off her. It was too late. She knew it was too late. "Oh God, Noah."

"Hmm," he murmured, obeying her frantic scrambling to get him off her. He withdrew from her body and collapsed on his back, his legs dangling over the edge of the bed. They'd been in such a rush to feel something other than pain, to push away the tears, that they'd fallen sideways across the full-sized bed. And they'd forgotten the most important thing.

"We didn't use a condom," she said.

He rolled onto his side and propped his head against his hand, his elbow pressing into the rumpled bedding. "Shit, I'm sorry," he said, his voice hoarse. Concern showed in his blue eyes. "I wasn't thinking straight, sweetheart. I can promise you I'm clean. I wasn't a saint these past five years, but I didn't screw around like some of the other guys."

She shook her head, not wanting to picture him screwing anyone else. Not right now while she was lying naked beside him, after he'd come inside her.

"I stopped taking the pill," she said, her voice hollow. How could she have let this happen? "I figured I wasn't great at remembering it anyway, seeing as I got pregnant. I meant to get an IUD. But I looked up the cost . . ."

"It's going to be OK." Noah drew her into his arms and she went, resting her head against his chest. He felt so strong, the muscles in his arms taut as they lay on the bed. "The chances are slim—"

"I can't lose another baby," she whispered.

"You won't." His hold tightened as if he could physically force the possibility away. "You could always take a morning-after pill before you leave for Germany."

"I could." But despite the bubbling fear, she couldn't bring herself to go to a doctor and ask to wipe away the possibility of a child. She couldn't lose another baby, not to a pill or an early delivery.

Of course, she wasn't in a position to have a child. But still, after fighting so hard for her baby to live, she couldn't erase another before he even had a chance . . .

"But," she began.

"You don't have to take anything, Josie. Whatever happens, we'll get through it. And you don't need to send a pigeon this time. I'm not going anywhere. And I'll be here when you get back from Germany."

She nodded, and the fear she'd pushed away for a few blissful—and potentially disastrous—minutes, returned. Her brother might be dying. She might never get to hear him laugh, or give her shit for, well, just about anything. And she might never get to see his expression when she told him she'd gotten naked with his best friend.

"It's going to be OK, Josie," he said as if he could make everything—Dominic, her potential pregnancy—A-OK through sheer willpower.

"Maybe."

She closed her eyes. *You can do this. You can face anything.*

She might be lying to herself. But she didn't have a choice. She needed to be strong because Noah couldn't rush in to play the hero this time. She'd found him reduced to tears, his emotions raw when she entered his room. He was in this with her.

With her head still resting against his chest, she wrapped her arm around him and held tight.

I'll be your anchor if you'll be mine, because if we send out a pigeon, I don't think anyone will rush to our rescue.

Chapter Nineteen

HER BROTHER, THE army ranger, had taken two rounds to the chest, penetrating the lungs and hitting a major artery. And a third bullet had shot straight through his hand. Now, machines surrounded him, their beeping oddly familiar.

Three bullet wounds require the same blinking, beeping machines as a premature baby.

Josie followed the lines on the screen tracking her brother's heartbeats. He'd survived two surgeries to repair the damage to his chest. She glanced at the long tube peeking out from under the hospital bedding. The tube ended in another machine, but it began in his left lung.

She looked up at him. A series of scratches covered one cheek. It looked as if he'd rubbed his face up against a rock. Fresh tears rolled down her cheeks. Her brother had tubes coming out of his chest, his hand was bandaged to the point it was unrecognizable, but the marks on his face brought her to tears.

"I held it together on the plane," she whispered. "I just sat there and hoped you would be OK. But then I realized that if you survive this, if you're fine, no permanent damage—you'll go back. I know you will."

Because Dominic had never been afraid. Or if he had been, he'd hidden it well. She'd only seen this desire to take on injustice, to fight for those who couldn't stand up for themselves. And his drive to be the best of the best. Her brother had his sights set on attending Ranger School from the beginning.

"Oh, Dominic," she said, raising her voice, hoping he'd hear her. But he hadn't opened his eyes since she'd arrived at the hospital. The nurse said that was normal given the anesthesia.

Normal.

She'd laughed, the sound brittle and bordering on hysterical. The nurse had left her alone with Dominic, but made sure Josie knew she'd be nearby in case anyone needed her. And she had a feeling the staff thought the recently arrived sister would need them more than the injured soldier.

But they didn't understand. She'd spent the longest and most precious weeks of her life sitting beside a hospital bed. It had been much smaller—technically an incubator—but the machines were the same. Watching the blinking lights on the monitors, waiting, that had become her normal.

And here she was again.

So much had changed. This was Dominic, not Morgan. She wasn't alone. Her father was asleep in the hotel room the army had arranged for their stay. But still, sitting here, watching someone she loved, a member of her family who owned a part of her heart that would shatter into tiny pieces if he didn't make it through just like it had when Morgan stopped fighting, she wondered . . .

What am I waiting for? Why am I pushing Noah away when I could be holding him close?

Her gaze remained fixed on her brother, but her mind wandered back to her hometown. To be fair, she had held him very close before they left. But reaching through grief, holding on to the person nearby to feel something, *anything* other than the fear wound tight to pain, that wasn't the same.

Watching Dominic's heartbeat on a computer monitor, she opened her eyes to the fact that she wanted Noah in her life. Yes, she was terrified that she couldn't handle the heartbreak if he decided to walk away, if he heard the words "I love you" and fled.

"The thing is," she murmured to her brother, "I think I love him."

She had run to Noah Tager's side when she'd needed someone. And this time, she hadn't been looking for him to step in and save the day. He couldn't do a damn thing for her brother. He wasn't a doctor. But he could bear witness to her pain and hold her close.

He'd changed over the past five years. She understood that, possibly better than anyone else in Forever. And she liked who he was now. He still possessed a body she wanted to explore, from his supersized muscles to his . . .

She glanced at her brother. The anesthesia still had a hold on him. But she didn't want him to wake up while she was thinking about Noah's abs. No, she needed to focus on his other qualities. The fact that Noah helped his friends when they asked. Sure, he didn't smile as much. But beneath his defensive scowl, she had a feeling he was still the same guy who'd driven his grandmother to the beach because she loved the feel of sand between her toes.

"I meant it when I told him I loved him that night. In the barn. Five years ago," she whispered. "I love him. Maybe I always have . . ."

And suddenly the thought of not risking her heart on Noah seemed so much worse than the potential fallout.

"HE'S GOING TO make a full recovery."

Noah heard those words, spoken over a crystal clear international connection, and he sank to his knees behind the bar. He'd been living in a fucking holding pattern for the past two weeks. Josie had called with updates, but never good news. He'd had to fight back tears after that first call, and he'd been working that time too.

"Dominic's here. I don't know much yet, but he was shot in the chest. He's in surgery." Josie had paused for what felt like forever. *"Again. But the nurse said most combat-related deaths happen before they reach the hospital, so all least he's here, right?"*

"Right," he'd confirmed as the pit in his stomach had turning into a fucking crater. And God, he'd felt like he *would lose it right there, one hand on the taps, his shoulder holding his phone pressed against his ear.*

"You all right down there?" Josh called from the other side of the bar. It was Tuesday and they'd just opened Big Buck's, otherwise Noah would have had a full audience to witness his weak-kneed tumble. "Not going to faint on me, are you? Because I left my smelling salts in the car."

He drew his cell away from his ear and looked up at the redheaded Summers brother peering down at him. "Shouldn't you be out somewhere chopping down trees and pissing off environmentalists?"

Josh shook his head. "Day off."

"Then sit down and drink your beer." Noah pushed himself off the ground.

"Noah, are you there?" Josie said.

"Yeah, I'm here."

"Dominic is going to be fine," she said. "Well, he'll probably never fight the bad guys again. The doctors said he did a number on his hand. And the pulmonary artery doesn't exactly heal overnight . . . But he's awake, breathing, and today he might get to eat something."

"I'm so fucking glad to hear that, Josie," he said, glancing at Josh. He had questions for her, but none that he wanted to ask in front of an audience. "Hold on a sec," he said to Josie. Then he covered the mic with one hand and spoke to Josh. "Mind going into the back to check on Caroline? She's been jumpy lately. I try to check on her every so often."

"Is she armed?" Josh asked casually as he slid off his stool and picked up his pint glass.

"No, her gun is still in my safe," he said.

Josh nodded. "Then it would be my pleasure."

Noah waited until the door to the back room swung closed, and then he removed his hand from the mic. "I'm back, Josie," he said, rounding the end of the bar and heading for the door. It wasn't anywhere near closing time yet. Hell, it wasn't even one in the afternoon. But he flipped the sign on the front door to closed.

"Everything all right there?" Josie asked.

"Yeah."

Except my dishwasher thinks she's being hunted and keeps asking for her gun back. Oh, and I miss you. The way you serve drinks like you own the place, the way you kiss, the way you feel beneath me, and hell, the way you call me a jerk.

"We're fine here," he continued. "How are you?"

"I'm glad that I flew over. Thank you for covering my bills. I'll pay you back. I promise."

"Paid sick leave, family leave . . . it comes with the assistant manager gig," he said.

Family leave.

She just might need that newly created benefit. He ran his hand over his face, closing his eyes. He'd spent the past two weeks coming to terms with the fact that part of him hoped she was pregnant. Shit, he'd put himself through fourteen straight days of pure hell, hoping that Josie would call him up and tell him they were having a baby. He wanted a reason to hold tight to her and not let go, an excuse to give Dominic now that his best friend was going to live—thank God—for wanting his little sister.

But shit, he was a jerk. How could he hope for something that would tear her apart? After what she'd suffered through the last time, it felt fucking selfish.

"Thank you," she said. "But I think I'm pushing the limits of sick leave even for the assistant manager."

"We'll talk about it when you get back," he said. *Please say you're coming home soon.*

"OK. But, Noah, I'm staying here until they send Dominic back to the States. My dad's leaving in a few days. He says he needs to get back to work. But I—"

"Take as long as you need," he said firmly.

"Thank you," she said, and this time her voice was soft and gentle. "When this is all over and Dominic is settled into a rehab hospital, then I'm coming home to you."

Noah opened his eyes and stared out into the empty bar. What the hell did that mean? Coming home to him or the bar, her job, and her debt?

"Hey, Noah?" Josh called, peering around the edge of the door to the back room. "Sorry, man, I didn't realize you were still on the phone."

"I'll let you go," Josie said.

"Bye. And, Josie, take care of yourself."

He lowered the phone, ended the call, and slipped his cell into his pocket. Turning his attention to Josh, he said, "What's up?"

"Your dishwasher is having a panic attack back here," Josh reported. "And it has nothing to do with the sparkling clean pint glasses."

Shit.

What could have happened since they arrived at the bar? They hadn't heard from Dustin since he sent that picture. Noah was close to convinced their former commanding officer wasn't hiding in his woods. So much so that he'd stopped searching the property after he closed the bar. Not that he was getting any more sleep. Most nights he lay awake thinking about Josie.

But he knew Caroline felt as if the threat was still imminent—from Dustin, from the police, who would arrest her if they found out she was AWOL. And while Noah was all for keeping her identity and the fact that she'd served alongside him in the marines out of the Forever gossip mill, he was starting to question if Dustin still posed a danger. Maybe their former commanding officer had given up. It wasn't much fun to torment someone who didn't respond. And the guy did have a family in California even if his wife had kicked him out.

"I'll talk to her," he said.

Josh stepped through the door and looked around the empty room. "Want me to man the bar? I think I can handle a crowd this size."

Noah raised an eyebrow as he lowered the wooden section dividing the back of the bar from the customer area. "We're closed. I already flipped the sign."

"Good." Josh's easy-going manner vanished. "You might want to keep it closed. That guy who's after her?"

Noah nodded, hearing the edge in Josh's voice. It sounded like the logger was taking Dustin's pursuit personally.

"He dropped off another picture," Josh continued.

"A printout this time. He must have slipped it under the door while she was unloading the clean dishes out front. Caroline didn't see or hear anything. And she's on her guard every damn second."

"Is the photo recent?" Noah demanded, his hand on the door, ready to push through and do whatever he needed to keep Caroline safe.

Maybe I can't do a damn thing for Josie or Dominic, but this I can handle.

"Yes," Josh said. "But the thing is, I'm not sure it is Caroline in the shot."

"What do you mean you're not sure?" he demanded.

"It looks a helluva lot like Josie."

A shiver ran down his spine, something he hadn't felt since he'd shouldered his weapon and headed out to face the bad guys.

"The picture was taken from a distance," Josh continued. "And they have the same long dark hair. Whoever took the shot could have made a mistake and thought it was Caroline."

"Where was it taken?" Noah asked. *Please don't say Big Buck's parking lot.*

"Caroline, Josie, whoever it is, she's standing outside your barn holding one of your kittens," Josh said, his tone grim.

Ah hell.

And just like that, Noah knew—his dishwasher had every right to be paranoid. Because this threat defined imminent danger. Dustin was out there. And he was close enough to see Noah's barn.

"We're keeping the bar closed," Noah said as he pushed through the door. "And we're going to find him."

THE SUN WAS slipping behind the clouds and Noah didn't have a clue where Dustin was hiding. He'd driven through Forever's quiet downtown with Josh and Caroline in his truck, scanning the streets. Josh had volunteered to pop into The Three Sisters Café and ask a few questions, and Noah had given him the go-ahead. The Forever town gossips didn't keep tabs on people who lived an hour or so away and were less likely to respond to Josh's questions with their own interrogation.

But Elvira hadn't seen a lone man fitting Dustin's description. No one had.

And their former commanding officer wasn't roaming the university campus. Noah had driven back and forth through the campus twice hoping to find Dustin hiding in plain sight.

Now they were walking through the woods between his property and the neighbor's land.

"We're losing the light," Noah said.

"We are," Josh acknowledged, stopping beside a fir tree. He stared up at it.

Noah turned to Caroline. Her lips were pressed together, her eyes darting to the blackberry vines and briar they'd been picking their way through for the past hour.

"You can admire my trees another time," Noah said. "But let's keep moving through this section. I'm pretty damn sure I'm the only one who has been crazy enough to walk through this overgrown area recently."

"Were you limbing last time you came through?" Josh asked, running his hand up the trunk.

"No, I haven't had a lot of spare time to remove branches and care for the damn trees. I was doing the same thing we're doing now only in the dead of night," he said. "Trust me, it's easier with the light. So why don't we keep walking while you lecture me on how to take care of my forest." He took a step toward Caroline.

"Someone's been climbing this tree with spiked boots." Josh continued to run his hand over the bark as he lifted his gaze to the tree's top. "And if you weren't limbing . . ."

"Hell." Noah marched over and stared at the tree trunk. He could see the marks from the spiked boots loggers wore to climb up and cut off the lower branches.

"Wait, he's been hiding in the trees?" Caroline said, scrambling to join them and turning her gaze skyward.

"He's not there now," Noah said. "We'd see him hanging from—"

Boom!

Noah grabbed Caroline and pulled her to the ground at the base of the tree. And Josh joined them, his movements lacking the all-hell's-breaking-loose panic Noah and Caroline carried with them like a souvenir of their last deployment.

"Not exactly hunting season right now," Josh said softly even though Noah had a feeling the shot had been fired from a distance.

"No, but someone's borrowing my neighbor's deer stand. The same damn one my dad fell from and broke his leg," Noah said, sitting up with his back against the tree Dustin had probably climbed at some point in the last few weeks. "I checked it out about a week ago. It was empty then."

"Not anymore," Caroline said. But she didn't appear nearly as shaken by the shot as the pictures. If Noah had to guess, he'd say she felt more comfortable with the certainty. Dustin was out there, in a stand positioned in a tree, and he was shooting at them. And it was a damn good thing the stand was far from their position. Noah only knew one marksman who could make that shot. Lena. But still, he wasn't willing to stand up.

"If we know where he is, let's go get him," Caroline said, pushing off the ground.

Noah pulled her back. "I don't think we should move closer. Most people can't make a shot at this distance, but Dustin's stupid enough to try."

"Or it was a warning," Caroline said, sinking back to the ground.

"Why would he reveal himself?" Josh asked.

"He wouldn't," Noah said flatly. "But if we approach the stand, we'll be within range. I think he's hoping we'll come closer."

"So what's the plan?" Josh patted the ground. "Camp here?"

Noah shook his head. "We'll go back the way we came. After dark." Because if they went the other way—toward the man hunting them—Noah couldn't guarantee Caroline's safety.

He stared out into the approaching darkness. For the first time in weeks, he was glad Josie was in Germany. But when she returned, how the hell was he going to keep her away from the insane ex-marine with the hunting rifle?

Chapter Twenty

"HOW ARE THE kittens?"

Josie had spent the last leg of her journey imagining what she would say when she walked through security at the Portland airport and into Noah's arms. *I've missed you. I want you. I think I'm falling in love with you.* But she'd taken one look at his tired face, the way he'd crossed his arms in front of his chest, and she'd gone with Plan B—*how are the freaking kittens.*

"Getting bigger every day. Caroline has been feeding them," Noah said, turning away from her and leading the way into the terminal. "Did you check a bag?"

She nodded and followed him onto the escalator leading down to the carousels. "How is Big Buck's best dishwasher?"

"She's on edge," he said flatly. "We had a scare a couple of weeks ago. The guy who's after her made it damn hard to ignore his presence."

She listened as he explained about the shot in the woods and the fact that the man who'd raped Caroline had vanished again after that.

"You should go to the police," she said. "My dad could help. We could explain about Caroline."

"Trust me, I've thought about it. But your dad wouldn't be doing his job if he didn't turn her in, Josie. And I can't send her back. She'll either end up in a cell or forced to work alongside men who blame her for ending Dustin's career. They'll harass her or worse." He opened the passenger side door and waited for her to climb in. "So please don't say anything to your father."

"I won't," she promised once he'd joined her in the cab of the truck.

"Thanks." Noah gave her a small smile, his first since she'd landed. He reached one hand out and touched her cheek. "I'm glad you're back. I've missed you. The bar's not quite the same without you."

She turned her head and pressed a kiss into the palm of his hand. "I missed you too."

They drove back to Forever, talking about the bar and Hoppy Heaven's wild success, and Dominic's recovery. Traffic remained steady and they didn't encounter a single box on the side of the road, filled with kittens or anything else. She didn't have an excuse to push him up against his truck and steal a kiss—and maybe more.

An hour and change later they pulled into her driveway and he put the truck in park. "Feel like giving me a hand with my bags?" she asked, keeping her voice light and playful. "Helping me sneak back into my dad's house?"

Noah raised an eyebrow, but kept his hands on the steering wheel. "I don't think it's a secret when he's expecting you."

"Good point, but he's not here now. He went in early today. So we could pretend. It might be fun."

"Fun." He looked at her as if he's forgotten the meaning of the word. Seeing that look, she knew they both needed a little break from the worrying.

"Noah." She looked him straight in the eyes. "I've been waiting for weeks to kiss you. So get your ass out of the truck and follow me inside." She opened the passenger door and hopped down.

Please follow me.

She heard a second truck door slam shut as she reached the side of the house, followed by the crunch of gravel beneath his boots.

"Naked kisses?" he demanded when he reached her side.

She nodded and headed for the back door. "I don't have an old mechanical bull here. Just a twin bed. Can you work with that?"

"Yeah," he said. But he stopped inside her kitchen.

She turned to face him, dropping her backpack and duffel on the floor. "There's no one here." She moved closed and placed her hands on his chest. "Just you and me."

"I know." He placed his hands on her hips and looked down at her, his blue eyes staring into hers. "But I still expect your dad or your brother to walk in. It feels wrong. Forbidden. And, sweetheart, that's not a turn-on. Not for me."

Her hope surged. He didn't want her because she was

off-limits. Kissing her, making love to her on that bull and in his bed had nothing to do with exploring what he couldn't have. He wanted *her*. She could feel it in the way his fingers pressed into her hips, holding her close as if he needed to keep her right there.

"I brought the toy Daphne gave me to Germany," she murmured. "Alone in my hotel room at night, I'd take it out, slip it beneath the sheets and pretend it was your cock."

"Josie—"

"But I have a secret." She rose up on her toes until her cheek touched his. She couldn't quite reach his ear. "The real thing is so much better."

"Josie," he growled, his hands sliding over her ass, moving lower to her thighs. He lifted her up and she wrapped her legs around him. "Josie, I love your dirty mouth."

Love. He'd said the word. She was tempted to whisper, *What else do you love? Me?* But she didn't want to push, not now, not yet.

He carried her up the stairs and headed straight for her room. Inside, he set her down and offered her a smile that was pure Noah.

"One, two, three," he began.

Her brow furrowed.

"Go!" he added as he pulled off his shirt.

Understanding dawned and she kicked off her sneakers, glad she'd left her boots in her closet. This time, she wanted to win the let's-get-naked contest. Except he'd already stripped off his pants, shoes, and socks.

When his boxers hit the floor, she paused, her thumbs hooked in her panties.

"Don't stop there," he said, walking around her and claiming a seat on her bed. He planted his feet hip-width apart, his erection ready for action. "I'm ready and waiting for you to climb up here and take me for a ride, cowgirl," he added. "Show me how you used your toy while you were away."

She slid her underwear down her legs and stepped out of them. Then she took a detour to her nightstand for a condom. "And what did you do while I was in Germany?"

He grinned and wrapped his hand around his cock, stroking from the base to the tip. She moved between his legs, watching his movements.

"I missed you, Josie."

She raised her gaze to his face. One look in his blue eyes and she knew he wasn't talking about wild, naked bull rides and orgasms.

I miss you.

It wasn't the same as "I love you," but she'd take it.

For now.

He reached for the condom. "We need to get this on now, or this will end before we get started," he added, his tone transitioning to light and teasing. But she could still hear the thread of need.

I miss you. I want you. I love you?

She hoped it was all there between them as she climbed up on the bed and straddled his hips. Replacing his hand with hers, she sank down onto his hard length. His gaze shifted to her breasts and he leaned forward, capturing one pert nipple between his lips. He put his six-pack to work, his hand gliding over her back as she started to move. She ground her hips against him and he let her take what she needed for a minute, maybe two, before he fought for control—and won.

This is the best kind of defeat.

But this time, as he pumped up into her, claiming control despite the fact that she was riding him—this time, she bit back the words "I love you." She knew it in her heart. But she refused to send him running for the door. She was willing to risk heartbreak, but she wasn't going to search it out today.

Maybe tomorrow. And when she did take that leap, she held tight to the hope he'd offer her the same words.

NOAH GROUND HIS teeth together and fought for control. There was so much they hadn't said to each other, things he need to ask, and more that he needed to tell her. Was she pregnant? When would she know? Because hell, he still wanted a reason to keep her close, to make her his.

But I should be pushing her away. What if I can't keep her safe? Dustin's still out there, always one fucking step ahead of me.

He lay back on her twin bed, his feet still planted on the floor. His head touched the wall behind him. The bed was so narrow. But he didn't give a damn. Not while he had his hands around Josie's hips, lifting and lowering her onto himself. He watched the full length of his dick disappear from view and felt her rub against him. He was tempted to reach between them and tease her, knowing it would give her the release she'd sought from her toy penis.

But he was a selfish ass. He wanted to draw this out. He wanted her here with him when he was pretty damn certain he should walk out the door and demand that she keep clear of him, Caroline, and the kittens in his barn, until he knew it was safe. Until he'd eliminated the threat of shots being fired . . .

"More, Noah," she demanded, arching her back. She raised her hands to her breasts and held them as she fought to ride him harder and faster . . .

"Josie," he murmured. He couldn't hold back. He was too close. The sight of her like this, riding him, taking everything he had to give . . . she blew the fantasies he'd carried with him for so damn long, to that hell in the desert and back, so far away . . .

"Tell me you're close," he demanded. "Because I can't—"

"Now," she moaned, her body shivering and convulsing above him. She stared down at him and he swore he saw her heart right there in her eyes silently offering the same words she'd given him five years ago—*I love you*.

He came hard and fast, closing his eyes to the rush of emotions. He shouldn't be here. He couldn't take her heart and promise to keep it safe. But he might walk away with it anyway.

Yeah, that made him a selfish jerk. Because soon, he might be forced to push her away. And it would break her heart.

Chapter Twenty-One

JOSIE HAD INSISTED on working last night in spite of her jet lag. She needed the cash. And she didn't want to be alone with her thoughts and the reality she'd been ignoring for the past few days.

She had to find a way to tell Noah how she felt. But that wasn't the only big reveal she had in store for the man who looked like he was already pushed to the limits.

The situation with Caroline was draining him. She could tell that he hated the waiting. He wanted to find Dustin first. But without going to the police—and after witnessing Big Buck's dishwasher's paranoia last night, Josie knew that wasn't going to happen—Noah didn't have much choice. Between his "strays" and the bar, Noah had been pushed to the edge.

Josie walked into The Lost Kitten's Toy Chest, inhaled the familiar scent of coffee and turned around. She'd made it to the parking area feeling as if she might lose her breakfast. She placed her hands on her thighs and bent over.

But she knew this feeling. The worst never happened, just loomed nearby, presenting a constant possibility.

"The toy chest inspires too many naughty thoughts first thing in the morning, huh?" Daphne said, moving to her side and running her hand over her back.

Josie braved an upright position and glanced at her friend. "It was the coffee, not the naughty nurse costumes and whips."

Her best friend's smile faded and her eyes widened. "Does that mean you're—"

"I'm pregnant." She doubled over again, wrapped her arms around her middle. But this time it wasn't nausea. Fear churned in her belly. How had she ended up here?

"Noah?" Daphne asked softly.

She nodded, but didn't stand upright. She wasn't ready. Not yet. "It's still early. Only four weeks. But I know."

"You took a test?"

"This morning." After she'd nearly thrown up her dad's eggs and bacon celebration breakfast. Her father's relief that Dominic would be all right, that he was coming home after rehab, probably to stay—it was palpable and led to large breakfasts. If only she had an appetite . . .

"At first, I told myself it was nerves. I came home planning to tell Noah that I love him, that I've fallen in love with him all over again. Or maybe I never stopped loving him." The words spilled out in a rush, aimed at the pavement covering the strip club parking lot.

"Whoa, wait," Daphne said, bending down to look at her.

"But I didn't tell him," Josie continued, pressing her eyes closed. "He looked so tired and overwhelmed by the past few weeks."

"Maybe he's been worried about you," Daphne said, placing a hand on Josie's back. "I'm guessing he knew this was a possibility."

"Maybe." But she knew it had more to do with Caroline and the man hunting them. "But I didn't tell him. I asked him to come in and . . . well, then at work last night, at the bar, the way he looked at me. I swear it's like he wants me, but still can't escape the guilt. For a guy who wants the world to think he's an asshole, it's kind of funny."

Josie let out a brittle laugh as she stood up and tried to see the humor. She struggled to feel better even as the ground felt like it was slipping out from underneath her. At this rate, she wouldn't be able to stand up on her own two feet much longer.

"Josie, come here." Daphne wrapped her arms around her and held her tight. "You have to tell him. How you feel, about the baby, everything. You've kept too much inside, trying to do everything on your own for so long. It's not possible and I won't let it tear you to pieces. Not this time."

"You're right," she whispered. "I'll tell him. Before the bar opens today."

"CAROLINE'S TAKING THE day off," Noah called as Josie walked into the bar. Her father had taken her Mini to the shop for a new starter while she'd been in Germany. Noah wished he'd thought to take that on too instead of leaving it to his best friend's dad. Chief Fairmore had enough on his plate. But he'd been so overwhelmed by the things he couldn't fix that he hadn't turned his attention to the things he could. "So we're on our own for dishes," he added.

"Is she OK?" Josie set her purse and apron on the bar and took a seat.

"Yeah." Noah focused on unloading the last rack of pint glasses. He'd come in early so that Caroline's absence wouldn't stretch his already overworked staff. April, the other bartender, had hugged him when he told her Josie was coming back to work. He suspected April thought he was holding out hope—and keeping a job open—for something that was never going to happen.

"I asked her to stay home today," he added. "It's been a few weeks since Dustin reached out." *And shot at us.* "I think it best if she lays low for a while. Plus I hired a private investigator to poke around down where Dustin's from in California. His wife and kids are still there, but no one's seen him in a while. Turns out his wife got a restraining order against him. So chances are he's still hanging around here somewhere, biding his time and trying to turn Caroline into a nervous wreck. Or more of a wreck. If that's his plan, it's working. She's losing it a bit."

And I don't want her anywhere near you. It's the only damn thing I can think of to keep you safe and out of range of a fucking shotgun and the woman who feels more and more like a cornered animal every damn day.

"We'll manage," Josie said, but there was a hefty dose of grim in her tone. "I'm sort of glad she's not here because we need to talk."

Noah set the pint glass down and looked at her. He knew what was coming. He'd been waiting, hoping to hear these words. Hell, he had to fight to keep from blurting out, *I know you're scared, but I want this. Our baby—*

"I love you," she said, and he took a step back. Yeah, he'd seen it in her beautiful, green eyes twenty-four hours ago when he'd been buried inside her. But he'd expected her to whisper the words with hope and passion, not the same voice she'd use to explain the details of Dominic's injuries.

He placed his hands flat on the bar. "Josie, I—"

"And," she continued, staring up at him, so damn determined to have her say that he shut up. And yeah, there wasn't much to say after her declaration. What the hell could he offer her in return? *I want you?* It wasn't the same.

"And we're having a baby," she said, her voice trembling.

Thank you, Jesus. He'd been waiting to hear those words, hoping he'd have a reason to turn to the world—

every damn person in this town, her father, her brother, everyone—and say, *She's mine. My family. My future.*

"You're sure?" he said, and damn, he sounded like a kid who couldn't quite believe Santa Claus had traveled down his chimney. It was too much a miracle to be true.

She nodded. "I took a test this morning."

He pressed his palms into the bar and pushed himself up, vaulting over the polished wood, scrambling to get to the other side, to reach her.

"Josie," he murmured, pulling her into his arms. He held her tight, clutching the damn happiness that had been thrust at him despite the problems that had come rushing in his direction, one after another.

How was he going to keep her safe? Dustin was out there and armed.

"I'm so scared," she whispered.

"Yeah, I know," he said. "I am too."

"I don't want to lose this baby," she added.

Forget Dustin. Those words, her feeling, her fears— this wasn't a madman he could hunt down in his freaking woods. There wasn't a damn thing he could do to keep her from losing this baby tomorrow or six months from now.

I can't take control and make everything all right.

There was no way around it. His arms fell to his sides and he pulled free from her hold, stepping away. He'd failed her the minute he'd let the grief carry him away, pushing him to take her without a condom. He'd delivered her back to the hell she'd fought so damn hard to escape. The pain. The grief. She might have to face all that again.

And there is nothing I can do about it.

He'd never felt so powerless.

But he could keep her out of the mad marine's range. He could steer her clear of Caroline—and, shit, himself.

"I want you to go home," he said firmly. "Rest. Tell your dad. Please, Josie, you're going to need his help this time."

"Wait. What?" she demanded, sinking back onto the stool. She wrapped her arms around her middle.

"I need you to leave," he said firmly.

"Noah, don't be stupid," she shot back. "I'm four weeks pregnant. I can serve drinks."

Noah shook his head. "Until I know that Dustin's gone, that he's not watching the bar, tracking me, or Caroline, that he won't start shooting again . . ." He couldn't bring himself to say "shooting at you," because he was never going to let that happen. "Until then, I need you to stay away from here. From me. And take care of yourself."

"But he's never shown up here," she protested. "This guy you think is after Caroline."

"What do you want me to say, Josie?" He placed his hands on his hips. "I can't take the risk that something will happen to you here. I'm not going to let you down. I'll be there for you and the baby. I'll do everything I can and that includes keeping you away from a madman with a gun. What else do you want?"

I WANT YOU to say that you love me too.

"I don't need a hero right now, Noah."

"Good. I'm not cut out for the role. Not anymore. I just need you safe—"

"And I need *you*." But even as she said the words, she knew it was hopeless. He was too afraid that he'd fail her. And too focused on the things that remained within his control. "I can't do this on my own."

"Ah hell, Josie, you don't have to," he said quickly. "I'll be there for every appointment. I'll make sure you have everything you need. I'm not walking away, Josie. I'm not like your ex. We're in this together."

"Everything I need," she repeated.

Everything but love.

And that was the piece she craved. She wasn't strong enough to get through this—the fear, the waiting, and the worrying—without someone's arms around her, holding her together. That's what she'd hoped for when she'd sat beside Dominic's hospital bed and decided to take a chance on Noah. She'd hoped for love. After everything that had happened, the guys she'd dated, the child she'd buried, she wanted to believe in love again.

"Everything," he repeated. "I just need to keep some distance until I know Dustin's been caught. After that, I'll take care of you. I promise—"

"If something goes wrong, if my water breaks again, there's nothing you can do," she said. "You know that, right? You can't stop it from happening. I've talked to half a dozen doctors and specialists. There's nothing they can do. Nothing anyone can do, but hope—"

"I know," he ground out. "Jesus, I know my hands are tied. I get that. So let me do what I can to keep you safe, all right?"

She saw the fear in his blue eyes. It mirrored hers. They might lose the baby. And it would destroy them both. She couldn't take on the grief and heartbreak. This wasn't the same as losing a boyfriend or watching the man you love leave to fight someplace so far away, where you can't quite picture the setting, never mind the day-to-day threats.

Losing Morgan had been one hundred times worse. She'd learned the ins and outs of helplessness, sinking deeper and deeper into the meaning of that word while she'd watched her baby struggle. And that feeling? True helplessness when faced with a loss that would crush your heart and soul? She knew it would just about kill Noah too.

But that didn't mean he had to shut his heart to the possibility of loving her. The only thing they could count on in this mess was love.

Except he didn't love her. Or if he did, he refused to say the words.

"You really are a jerk," she said, her voice trembling as if she might break into tears. But anger held them back. "It wasn't just a show to keep everyone around here from patting you on the back, was it?"

His mouth formed a thin line and he nodded. "Yeah, I am, Josie. But I'm the jerk who is going to keep you safe."

"It's not enough," she said softly, the pain in her chest slowly filling out and taking shape.

"It's all I've got."

Chapter Twenty-Two

"HE'S OUT THERE, Noah. I know he is."

Noah leaned back against the bar and looked over at Caroline. His conversation with Josie had left him with a hollow, panicked sensation circling his chest. But he'd barely had time to think about whether pushing Josie away was the right thing to do before Caroline showed up at the bar with news that left him questioning damn near everything.

"If Dustin's here," he said slowly, "why did the private investigator send proof that he was in California?"

Caroline had used his dad's computer to check her email and learned the guy Noah'd hired in California had found Dustin alive and well. Yeah, the scumbag was stalking his ex-wife, which violated the restraining order Dustin's ex had filed. But there was no sign their former CO had followed Caroline to Oregon.

Caroline threw her hands up in the air and began

pacing the empty bar. As soon as she'd arrived, Noah had locked up even though he'd only opened for business five minutes earlier.

"Maybe he drove back," she said. "It's been weeks since he shot at us."

"In his email, the investigator said he spoke with Dustin's ex-wife. Dustin's been bothering her ever since she got the order. She's placed a handful of calls to the police."

Caroline stopped in the middle of the room. With her hands on her hips, her long hair flowing over her shoulders and her expression turned to pissed-as-hell, Caroline looked a helluva lot like the last woman who'd left this bar. Except the angry marine wasn't about to declare her love.

And Noah didn't feel the same all-consuming need to keep Caroline safe. He wasn't about to let her get shot or locked up again. But with Josie . . . the thought of anything happening to her . . .

Crazy, wild panic. He felt it pulsing through him.

"If it wasn't Dustin," Caroline challenged, "then who shot at us?"

"I don't know." And yeah, that fact drove him close to crazy too.

"Maybe it's one of the guys," she said. "Someone who served with us and blames me for pressing charges against his beloved CO."

"Could be," Noah agreed, reaching for his phone. "I'm going to call April and see if she can come in and cover the bar. Then I'd like to walk the woods around the barn and have a close look at that hunting stand."

He made the call, promising April a Saturday night

off with pay if she'd come in now. And thirty minutes later, he climbed into the driver's seat of his truck while Caroline buckled her seat belt.

"I heard you tell April that you might not make it back before closing," Caroline said as they turned out of the parking lot.

"I'm going to find this bastard tonight. Or hell, at least find out who has been sending the pictures." He glanced over at Caroline. "I don't want you always looking over your shoulder."

She left out a rough bark of laughter. "Finding him won't erase my paranoia, Noah. If I'm discovered here, I could be arrested. That threat won't go away and you can't change that."

"I wish I could," he ground out. "You don't deserve to live like this. Hiding and afraid."

"But that's life. And, Noah, it's about time you realize that there are some things you can't change. You can't always save the day."

He pressed on the brakes as they approached a red light. "You're the second person today who has tried to drive that point home."

"Josie?" Caroline said.

He nodded.

"Did you listen?"

"Right now keeping her safe is my top priority," he said gruffly.

"Then your priorities are messed up."

"You really are losing it," he murmured as he hit the gas and they sped toward his childhood home.

"Noah, I'm more than what happened to me. I've been in love."

He cast a glance at her. "Josh?"

"No." He saw her shake her head out of the corner of his eye. "I can't love him. Not now. But before I joined the marines, before everything, I had a boyfriend. The relationship didn't survive the first deployment, but still . . . I know you should be focused on *why* keeping Josie safe comes first in your life," Caroline said.

Noah stared at the empty two-lane road. "I can't lose her. I let her go once and I spent five years wishing I was with her. And now . . . I don't want to be a hero. But I need to save her."

"From the madman with the gun?" Caroline asked softly.

"From everything. I just need her to be OK."

"Impossible."

"I know." He turned onto his drive. "And it's killing me."

Because I love her.

He'd always loved her. But this time, he'd fallen hard for her. Yet, Caroline was right. If he loved her, he had to face that fact he couldn't protect her from everything.

Except the madman hunting them. Please, God, let him keep her safe from whoever the hell was after them.

JOSIE STEERED THE Mini toward home, feeling as if her world had been turned upside down. The one person she'd thought she could trust, the one who had promised to always rush to her rescue, had pushed her away. For her safety! How had she ended up back here? Broken-hearted because Noah didn't love her.

This time felt different. I saw the love in his eyes.

But if he did love her, it wasn't enough to overcome his need to focus on the things he could control—like her freaking safety.

She parked in front of her house but didn't reach for the door. Should she go back and try to talk to Noah again? Even though he hadn't said the words, she knew she wasn't strong enough to face this pregnancy alone.

"Josephine?"

Her father stood outside the Mini, peering in the driver side window. She'd been so wrapped up in her questions—Go back? Move forward alone?—that she hadn't heard her dad approach.

"I thought you were working today," her father said. "Is everything all right?"

She opened the door and climbed out of the car. "No, Dad." Closing the door, she met her father's concerned gaze. "I fell in love with Noah. I'm pregnant."

"Pregnant?" He father's eyes widened.

Her lower lip trembled. "And I'm scared. I can't lose another baby. I can't do this on my own. I can't."

"Josie." Her father wrapped his arms around her and held her tight. "Another . . . another baby?"

She nodded, her cheek pressed against the stiff, starched surface of his police uniform as his hold tightened.

Then he released her and took her hand. "Come inside. I'll make you some eggs."

She allowed her father to lead her up the back porch steps and into the kitchen. She'd expected an interrogation right there in the driveway. But he didn't look disappointed or disapproving. She glanced at his weathered face. The sadness etched into the deep lines on his forehead, into his grey-green eyes, nearly knocked her off her feet.

"I'm sorry, Daddy."

He pulled out a chair from the kitchen table and held it for her. "I think I'm the one who should be apologizing. For your loss. For not being there."

"I didn't tell you." She sank into the chair.

"I'm listening now," he said. "Why don't you start at the beginning and I'll make the eggs?"

She nodded and started talking, explaining about her stupid ex, the way he'd left, how her water broke too soon. By the time she started describing Morgan's final days, tears streamed down her father's face as he stood over the stove. She explained why she needed to repay the hospital and doctors while he plated their breakfast.

She'd told him everything by the time he set the dishes on the table. Almost. She'd left that night in Noah's barn years ago, or how she'd fallen for him this time, out of the story. And she skimmed over the depth of her depression after losing Morgan.

"Josephine." He withdrew a handkerchief from his back pocket and wiped his eyes, but the tears continued to fall. "I'm sorry you felt you had to hide this from me."

"I thought I could do it on my own," she said, her voice shaking. "And I didn't want to return home a failure."

"Things would have been different if your mother had lived. I wouldn't have fought to control you." He shook his head. "But I can't change the past. I wish I could, but . . ."

"Me too." She wouldn't hand back the few weeks of Morgan's life. Not for the world. But if she could go back, she'd hold on to her heart and stay away from Noah's barn and his bed. She'd listen to her fear—she couldn't handle the aftermath—instead of pushing back against it.

"But this time"—he covered her hand with his—"you're not alone. I'm here. And Noah is a good man."

"He is," she acknowledged slowly. "But he's not ready to love me. He knows about Morgan . . ." Her father flinched at the sound of his late wife's name even though she'd already told him that she'd named the baby after her mother. "And I don't think Noah is ready for . . . for . . . what could happen."

"I'll talk to him," he father said firmly.

"You can't make him love me," she said. "And there's a chance I'll lose this baby too. The thought of something so far beyond his control terrifies him. I know it scares me. So much."

"You can't let fear prevent you from living," he said. "And neither can Noah."

"It's not that simple. There are other factors." She stabbed the eggs with her fork. She couldn't expose Caroline. Sure, Josie had been through hell and heartbreak. But Caroline had endured much worse.

"Either you talk to him or I will," her father said.

"No—"

"Look at what you've survived, what you've over-come," he said. "I know grief. It's not easy. But you're strong enough to move past it. And so is Noah. If you love him, go talk to him." Her father looked her straight in the eyes. "Don't let the person you love run away because he's afraid—or you are. Trust me, every day counts."

She set her fork down. She thought of how Morgan had felt in her arms . . . how her mother had breathed life into their home . . . and how her father had looked at her mother, his usually reserved expression so filled with love . . .

"You're right, Dad. I'll go talk to him."

And this time I won't let him push me away for "my safety."

She refused to let a madman with a chip on his shoulder keep her from being with the man she loved. And if Noah pushed her away again? If he refused to love her back?

She'd survive. Her father was right. She couldn't hide behind fear that she couldn't handle the outcome—not when it came to her relationship with Noah, or her baby.

Chapter Twenty-Three

FIGHTING FOR LOVE, or even a second chance to say those words and demand to know how Noah felt—not his determination to keep her safe, but what was in his heart—required finding him.

He wasn't at the bar. She'd stopped by and found April in charge. And he wasn't at the house. Josie had said hello to his dad before heading back to the parking area where her Mini stood beside his truck. Holding tight to her determination, she marched across the gravel and headed for the barn door.

The kittens greeted her as she flipped the light switch. Overheard, the fluorescents illuminated the mechanical bull in the corner.

"Ouch!" She glanced down and found a pair of kitten-sized claws digging into her Converse sneakers. The stupid shoes were too old and worn to protect her feet from a playful fur ball.

"Crying with pain?" a familiar voice jeered. "I haven't touched you yet."

She looked up and froze, her gaze locked on the shotgun's long barrel. It was the second time she'd had a gun pointed at her in Noah's barn. But the man holding the shotgun was twice Caroline's size. And he wasn't a crazy former marine. She knew him.

"Travis," she said slowly. "Please put the gun down."

"It figures you'd be here," he said without lowering the weapon. He stood on the faded cushion, the bull at his side like a mechanical sidekick. "Always with him, aren't you? At the bar. In his barn."

Always with who? Noah?

She struggled to put the pieces together. Why, after all this time, would Travis come after her? She'd barely seen him since she'd returned home. Not after Noah kicked him out of the bar.

But he'd seen her. He'd been watching them. Her. Noah. Caroline.

"You're the one who sent the pictures," she murmured. "And you shot at Noah."

"You didn't even see me up in that hunting stand. I would have made the shot if you hadn't played chicken, hiding behind the tree."

I wasn't there.

He'd mistaken Caroline for her.

"You were after me," she said, her hands trembling. Oh God, after all these years, her pissed-off, hot-tempered ex had been hiding out, hunting for her. It felt as if her life was spiraling out of her control. Maybe Noah was right to fear the things that were far beyond his power. She'd been so sure someone was searching for poor, paranoid Caroline.

"Not you," he sneered, keeping the barrel pointed at her. "I'm here for Noah. He's humiliated me one too many times. Starting rumors. After he broke my nose, I couldn't get a job. Did he tell you that? Word got out that I had anger issues. I couldn't pay for school. Now who do you suppose started those rumors?"

Someone you hurt? Someone you hit?

She'd never breathed a word. Noah was the only witness. But now she wished she'd spoken up. How many women had he hurt? How many girlfriends fell for him and then stepped back in shock when he unleashed his anger? Had they blamed themselves? Or started spreading rumors . . .

"It wasn't Noah," she said.

"He kicked me out of Big Buck's. I come in for one damn shot. A chance to welcome you home—"

A shudder ran down her spine. She didn't want his welcome. But she'd never suspected it would lead to this.

"He refused to serve me in front of the whole fucking bar because you ran away from me," Travis continued, his grip tightening on the shotgun. "Let's see how much of a hero he is when I point a gun in his face."

"If you want to find out," Noah called from behind her. The sound of his voice moved along with the click of his work boots on the barn's cement floor. "You'd better aim that thing at me."

NOAH STARED AT the shotgun as the truth sank in. Night after night, he'd been chasing a threat that didn't exist. He'd been convinced Dustin had followed Caroline to Oregon. But Dustin wasn't out there. And Travis Taylor, the man he'd fought five years ago, didn't want a piece of the AWOL marine—he wanted Noah.

Come and get me, asshole.

He would do anything to keep that gun aimed at him. Anything to keep Josie safe.

"You want to see me cower?" Noah challenged again, his gaze locked on Travis. His heart raced, beating faster and faster each second the gun remained aimed at Josie. "I'm your target, Travis. I'm the one to blame. Point the gun at me."

The shotgun cut through the air. Travis held it steady, his dark eyes glistening with excitement. Noah knew that look. He'd witnessed it while deployed—on both sides of the battle. Travis wanted to hurt.

Don't hurt Josie.

"Take your shot, man," Noah called. Keeping Travis's attention on him—that was the only element he could control. Everything else about this clusterfuck was out of his power.

I'm not going to let you down, Josie. I'm going to keep my promise. I'll keep you and the baby safe.

He heard a soft gasp, but didn't risk looking at Josie. One glance might draw Travis's attention back to her. And yeah, he was close to counting his lucky stars that he'd sent Caroline up to the house after they'd hiked out to the hunting stand, hoping to find a clue. A paranoid marine wouldn't add to this equation. Plus, he wanted her out of range. Josie too.

Go to the door, Josie.

He sensed movement, but he resisted the urge to steal a glance.

"You have me, Travis," he said, raising his hands palms up in a show of surrender.

"Some war hero," Travis said with a laugh.

Beneath the sound of his voice, Noah heard the soft roar of a machine coming to life.

What the hell are you doing, Josie? Why aren't you running?

"I'm not a hero," Noah said, allowing some of the panic he felt to slip into his words. "Not even close."

I'm scared. So damn afraid of the things I can't change.

The bull spun on its axis. The horns whirled toward Travis, who'd chosen to remain at the machine's side, probably using the old cushions to gain a few inches above Noah. But the power of the old bull was no match for Travis.

The man who'd pushed Noah to the edge, who'd left him walking around so damn worried that he'd been ready and willing to push the woman he loved out of his life if it meant keeping her in one piece—Travis fucking Taylor fell back on his ass and the gun went flying.

God bless that bull.

Noah raced forward and scooped the shotgun off the matt. And then he looked up at the woman manning the bull's controls. No, he wasn't the hero here. It was Josie.

"What the hell were you thinking?" he demanded as he stood over Travis, the gun pointed down at the man who'd served up so much damn trouble.

"I thought someone needed to jump in and save you," Josie shot back. "And that someone had to be me."

Chapter Twenty-Four

NOAH WATCHED JOSIE scoop up a mewing fur ball outside his barn and head over to the porch steps. They'd pulled the kittens from the barn when the police showed up, led by Josie's father, and declared it a crime scene. Now, they were waiting for the men in blue to wrap up.

Movement diverted his gaze and he turned his head to witness the deputy escort a handcuffed Travis to a police cruiser. The car door slammed and he turned his attention back to Josie, who was now carrying two kittens and heading straight for him.

He'd failed to keep her safe. The situation had gotten out of hand and she'd come to his rescue. Yeah, he was pretty sure he'd failed the hero test big-time. Not that he'd wanted the label. Still, he wished he could have kept her far away from Travis's gun.

But Caroline was right. He needed to look at why he was hell-bent on keeping her safe. Because Josie had made it pretty damn clear she didn't need someone rushing to her rescue. Yeah, she'd told him as much this morning. But there was nothing like watching the woman he loved defeat an armed madman to drive the point home.

The woman I love. It's about time I tell her.

"You know what you forgot to say back there?" Josie said, coming to a halt in front of him.

"Thank you?" he said mildly, cocking his head as he looked up at her.

"You can do better than that." She claimed a space beside him on the porch step.

"Thank you for saving my ass," he said.

"You're welcome. But as much fun as that was, I'll be happy if no one ever points a gun at me again in that barn," Josie said, settling the purring kittens onto her lap.

Noah reached over and took her hand. "I'll make damn sure of it."

"Don't make promises you can't keep," she said softly. "You can't post a sign outside saying 'No Crazy Gun-Wielding People Allowed.' Especially with Caroline living here."

"I'm hoping she might relax now that we have proof it wasn't Dustin after her."

"Where is she?" Josie asked, glancing back at the house.

"Josh came by and picked her up while you were giving your statement. I called and asked him, thinking it would be best if she wasn't here right now. Too many cops and she's still on edge."

"She's not the only one," Josie murmured. "My stomach is still doing flips from the sight of Travis holding a shotgun."

He turned and looked right at her. "You can relax now. You took out the bad guy. You were incredible, using the bull like that."

"Now that you have proof that you don't need to keep me safe, if anything I should be the one looking out for you," she said, speaking quickly as her green eyes stared into his. "Now that's off the table, Noah, I need to know—"

"That I lied to you earlier," he cut in. "I told you that keeping you safe . . . I said that was all I had to give, but I lied."

"A jerk and liar," she murmured. "Not a great combination."

"I'm nowhere close to perfect. Trust me, I know that. But I also know that I love you, Josephine Fairmore." He released her hand. "I want you to save me from trouble— real or imagined—every chance you get for as long as you'll have me."

I LOVE YOU, Josephine Fairmore.

Driving over here, facing her crazy, gun-wielding ex—it had all been worth it to hear those words. She could have done without the showdown in the barn, but still, it was worth it.

"Forever. This time, I'm going to keep you forever. *We're* keeping you forever." She placed her hand on her belly, and Noah glanced down. "I can't promise we won't bring trouble to your barn door again."

"We can take on trouble." He raised his gaze to her lips. "Anything beyond my control, I know you'll handle." His palms cupping her cheeks, he leaned close and pressed his lips to hers. One sweet, heated kiss before he drew back. "I'm not walking away from you again, Josie. No matter what happens, I'm going to stay by your side, loving you."

Josie closed her eyes and rested her forehead against his. Life had handed her one barrier after another. Unexpected pregnancy. Preterm labor. The loss of her baby. A second unplanned pregnancy . . . She hadn't felt strong in a long time.

Until now.

She'd risked her heart, opened herself up to love again, and this time she'd found happiness. Sure, she'd had to fight for it. But she'd won. Now, she was stronger, happier, and wildly, madly in love.

"I love you, Noah." She leaned back and took his hand, placing it over her still-flat stomach. "And whatever the future brings, I know we can face it together."

Epilogue

JOSIE CRADLED THE sleeping infant in her arms. She was small, born at just thirty-four weeks, but healthy.

Perfect. She's absolutely perfect.

"Can't stop staring?"

She glanced up from her little girl to the man leaning against the doorway, holding a pair of steaming to-go cups. Noah had rushed her to the hospital after her water broke and stayed by her side, holding her hand while she screamed from the torturous mix of pain and panic.

Over and over she'd told him she couldn't do this. And he'd told her that he loved her and that he believed in her. She'd seen the fear in his eyes, for her, for the baby. But he'd stayed and fought through it with her.

And her baby—their daughter—was born.

"Is that coffee?" she whispered, not wanting to wake the baby.

"Hot chocolate for you," he said, stepping into the room. "I wasn't sure if you could have caffeine."

"Thanks," she said, nodding to the nightstand beside her hospital bed. He walked in and set one of the cups down. He looked down at their child and smiled. There was so much love in his eyes . . .

Oh God, she was going to cry from the potent mix of exhaustion, hormones, and emotion.

"Did you call Dominic?" she said.

He nodded and his expression turned serious. "I did. He should be coming home soon. It sounds like the rehab facility plans to release him next week."

"He'll get to meet his niece." She glanced down at the sleeping baby, then back up at Noah. "Worried he'll take a swing at you for getting me pregnant?"

"No," Noah said, brushing a kiss to her forehead. "I'll let him throw a punch or two if he wants. Because falling for you? Getting you pregnant?" He leaned over their sleeping baby and gently kissed her. "Worth it."

"She's perfect, isn't she?" Josie said as he straightened. "I was worried . . . she wasn't as early, but still."

"You were amazing, Josie. I know you were scared, but you did it. You were so strong. Hell, half the time I was certain you didn't need me."

"Just your love," she said softly.

The baby stirred in her arms and she glanced down. But her perfect little girl was sound asleep.

"Josie." She looked up and saw the smile she remembered from five years ago on his face. "I'm going to love you forever. And our little girl too."

A barn, a mechanical bull, his best friend's
off-limits sister,
and an oh-so-bad-it's-good idea.
If you missed it, here, in its entirety, is

RUNNING WILD

the prequel that kicked it all
off for Noah and Josie!

Chapter One

June 2012

NOAH TAGER SWERVED and avoided burying his pickup in the big blue mailbox on the sidewalk. *Thank you, Jesus.* He threw his truck into park and cut the engine. The street sign on the far side of the mailbox read "No Standing." But leaving his dad with a parking ticket beat a totaled truck. And he had a feeling Forever's Finest, the police force that patrolled the Oregon college town, would forget all about the ticket when he called for their help.

Chief Fairmore? I saw Travis Taylor lead your daughter into the alley beside The Three Sisters Café where he tried to introduce his palm to Josie's face. Not his fist. No, the asshole went for the open-handed slap.

Through the windshield, he'd seen Josie Fairmore pull her hand free from her soon-to-be ex-boyfriend and block the slap. Noah had been too busy trying not to hit the mailbox to see if Travis had tried again.

But Chief Fairmore wouldn't give a damn if his little girl's boyfriend failed to connect with his target. And her brother? Dominic would jump at the chance to have a physical "conversation" with the asshole who had helped Josie earn her reputation as the town bad girl. Although he knew she wasn't as "bad" as certain gossips led everyone to believe. Just a little wild.

Noah slammed the door to his truck and ran down the sidewalk toward the alley. Oh hell yeah, he was ready and willing to fight alongside the Fairmore men. Starting right now in the alley.

But a cloud of gloom and doom followed, hovering over his head. It rained questions as he reached the gap between the two-story historic buildings.

Was this the first time? Had Travis tried this before? Why the hell had Josie stayed with Travis's sorry ass after the incident during the homecoming parade? After Travis had allowed the blame to fall on her shoulders?

Noah ground his teeth together. He'd talked Dominic out of throwing a punch—or ten—after Forever's gossip-prone triplets, the owners of The Three Sisters Café, had stumbled upon Travis and Josie in the back of the hay wagon. It was bad enough everyone would be talking about the fact that Travis, the quarterback and hero of the hour, had been caught with Josie's black silk panties in one hand. Beating the younger kid up would only add fuel to the gossip mill, Noah had told his friend.

Plus it wasn't a fair fight. Travis was just a kid. Eighteen. And without his offensive line, Travis didn't stand a chance.

But now Noah wished he'd kept his mouth shut and thrown a punch or two back then himself. He wouldn't hesitate to use his fists today.

He rounded the corner and spotted Josie.

But Travis was gone.

Goddamn coward.

Noah froze on the edge of the pavement, one step short of entering the narrow, gravel-covered space between the two buildings. Josie stood with her back pressed against the cement wall, her head held high and her eyes open. He had banished the words "Dominic's sister is freaking hot" from his vocabulary not long after Josie started high school. But he wasn't blind. She possessed the kind of beauty that dared men to look away. Her long legs and curved hips could have walked her straight into a modeling career.

Except small-town Oregon wasn't exactly bustling with scouts looking for the next cover girl. And even if someone saw her and offered her a contract, it would probably be a one-way ticket to the cover of *Sports Illustrated*'s swimsuit issue.

He'd witnessed Josie in a barely there bikini once. Yeah, he'd silently thanked the genius that had invented the two-piece swimsuit. Then he'd spent the rest of the pool party staring at his feet or talking to his friends—

anything but looking at Josie Fairmore long enough to want what he could never have.

Right now, in the alley, it wasn't her curves, barely hidden by her fitted spaghetti-strap tank top and jean cutoff shorts that stunned him. He'd left his truck planning to pull Travis off her. He'd expected to find her radiating fear. Travis had failed to lead his team to the state championship, but as quarterback that guy was still big. The threat of a slap from a man that size would inspire some serious terror.

But eighteen-year-old Josie Fairmore wasn't cowering and calling for help. She stood with her feet planted hip-width apart, arms at her side, and stared straight ahead. Her body language screamed *don't mess with me*.

He studied the red mark on her left cheek. Travis Taylor hadn't received the message.

When I get my hands on him. . .

Even though she appeared calm and in control, her palms pressed against her outer thighs, the rise and fall of her chest betrayed her. His best friend's little sister was five seconds away from hyperventilating in the alley.

"Josie," he said. The gravel crunched beneath his cowboy boots as he stepped toward her.

She turned to him, her dark eyes widening. And there it was—the fear—piercing, sharp, and directed at him.

Oh no, Josie, no. Discovery is not your enemy here.

"Hey, Noah." She forced a smile. Her voice was low and rough, bordering on sultry. Or maybe that was his imagination. "Any chance we could pretend you didn't see me today?"

"No." His tone a helluva lot sharper than he intended. "I have to be honest, Josie. I'm seconds away from speed-dialing your dad at the station, followed by your brother."

Her smile vanished, leaving behind a mask of worry. "Calling the cops because I snuck out on a Saturday afternoon? I don't think they can arrest me for not listening to my dad. I've been grounded for the past three weekends. I had to get out."

Snuck out?

And what the hell was up with her raspy voice? Was she trying to charm him into pretending he hadn't nearly crashed his truck when he spotted her?

"I saw Travis." He struggled to keep his tone level and kind. The last thing she needed was another big guy offering hostility. Sure, it had been four years since Noah had traded his quarterback jersey for a job at his dad's struggling country western bar, but he still had the strength and height to hurl the ball a lot farther than the damn kid who'd hit her.

I'm going to fucking kill Travis Taylor.

It was one thing to suspect, to nearly hit a mailbox hoping he was seeing things or that he'd get there in time to stop the asshole from raising his arm a second time. But to see the proof on Josie's face? Noah would hunt the town's hero of the hour down and make him hurt. Shit, he'd probably land his ass in jail for his trouble. And earn a dishonorable discharge before he even set foot in basic training.

Was that even possible? Could the marines kick him out before he arrived? Would going after Travis wipe away his chance to earn the steady paycheck his family needed to stay afloat?

"He's kind of the reason I slipped out of the house," she said, raising her right hand to her neck. "I needed to talk to him. We're going to different schools in the fall. I thought it would be better if we ended things now. He'll be here and I'll be in Portland."

"You're breaking up with Travis because of the *distance*?" This time he couldn't keep the heavy dose of *what the fuck* out of his voice. Portland was only an hour, maybe two with traffic, from the Willamette Valley.

"That was my plan," she murmured.

"Just because he didn't want to break up, that doesn't give him the right to—"

"I know," she said sharply, her hand still rubbing her neck.

His gaze narrowed, studying the way her long black hair fell over her shoulders. Her pale skin offered a stark contrast to her dark locks. Except around her neck. The area beneath her fingers appeared red. He had to look hard to see it. But a series of scratch marks stood out against the creamy white skin. As if she'd been trying to tear something away from her neck—or someone. Like the person who'd left behind those angry red marks.

"Ah hell, Josie." He moved closer and drew her into his arms. At first it was like hugging a two-by-four length of wood. But gradually, she relaxed and wrapped her arms around him. And he just held her, not trusting himself to speak. If he opened his mouth now words like "I'm going to make sure no one ever hurts you again" would tumble out. But he couldn't make that promise. He couldn't stay by her side, ready and willing to save the day. His dad and grandmother were depending on him to show up at basic training and go wherever the hell the marines needed him.

"Please don't tell anyone," she whispered, her cheek against his shoulder. "Not my dad. And please promise me you won't breathe a word about this to Dominic."

"Josephine." He drew back and looked down at her. "Travis hurt you. He deserves to rot in a cell for what he did."

"It's his word against mine," she said softly.

"I saw him," he ground out. "His hand raised above you—I saw him."

"You're leaving in two weeks. And then it will be just the same as it was after the homecoming dance when we were caught in the hay wagon."

"What?" His brow furrowed. He couldn't draw the parallel between two teenagers discovered in a somewhat compromising position—and they'd both had most of their clothes on—to a two-hundred-pound man slapping his girlfriend and wrapping his hands around her neck.

"Everyone saw Travis holding my underwear and thought, 'Boys will be boys,'" she said. "But then they looked at me and thought, 'Slut.' I swear there are still some people in this town who think I hypnotized him with my breasts and made him follow me to that wagon. He couldn't help himself. And it will be the same thing this time. They'll take one look at me and think, 'No! Not our football star!'" She delivered those words in a familiar high-pitched, condescending tone.

"Josie—"

"Face it, Noah. As soon as you leave, Travis will take your place as the town Golden Boy. He'll be the hero everyone pats on the back. They'll tell the story of his winning touchdown at that game leading up to the state championship over and over just like they told yours."

"We won state my year," he pointed out. But after four years, the thrill of the win had faded. He hadn't been able to afford college. And while he'd been the best in a small town, he wasn't good enough for a full scholarship. He stayed in Forever along with his two best friends, all lost in a town they'd lived in their whole lives.

Now they'd finally settled on something. Military service. A career with purpose, challenge, and a steady paycheck. They were going to do something good and become heroes for something other than throwing a piece of pigskin.

"Travis will be untouchable," Josie continued. "And I'll still be . . . me."

"There is nothing wrong with you," he said quickly, wishing like hell she hadn't hit the nail on the damn head with her summary of Forever, Oregon.

Sure, not everyone tossed Travis up on a pedestal. But most did. Football had a tight grip on the town. He knew that better than anyone. He'd spent years on his podium in the clouds. And yeah, it might have gone to his head if he hadn't faced the day-to-day struggles of life with a widowed father working to make ends meet for him and his grandmother.

"There's plenty wrong with me," she shot back. "I'm

stubborn, headstrong, and my best friend's mother owns a strip club outside of town. Oh, and I like sex."

"Nothing on your list points to a character flaw," he said, lumping every bullet point together, not wishing to point out that "I like sex" was definitely in the plus category as far as he was concerned. But if her brother heard those words, he'd probably have a different opinion. And Noah should be approaching this situation—and any other that involved Josie—as if she were his kid sister.

She pulled away, stepping out of his reach. "I need your word," she said, wrapping her arms around herself. "That you won't tell anyone."

"Three conditions." He folded his arms across his chest in a pose that mirrored hers. "First, you stop seeing him."

"Done," she said. "I'll tell him again and again until he gets the message."

He shook his head. "No. You can call him. But I'll make sure he understands. That's my second condition. I'm going to have a chat with your soon-to-be ex."

She nodded.

"Third condition," he said, knowing this one would be tricky. "If you ever land in a situation you can't handle, call me."

She let out a raspy laugh. "And you'll what? Ride in on your white horse and save me? From Afghanistan? Or Iraq? Or wherever else they're sending recently enlisted marines these days?"

"Call, email, or send a letter. Hell, send a carrier pigeon. I don't care how you get in touch, or where I am.

If you need me, I'll find a way to help. It doesn't matter where I am or what I'm doing. You're like family to me, Josie. And I'm always here for you."

"Like family?" She raised an eyebrow. "So you're doing this for Dominic? Because my brother is your BFF?"

"No, I'm doing this because I care about you," he growled.

She stepped back and he wished he'd kept those words locked away. Let her think this was all about his best friend, her brother. But no, he had to toss out the "c" word, which in teenage speak probably held almost as much weight as "like" and, God help him, "love."

"Like family," she repeated.

And he nodded even though he had a feeling she was running through every look he'd ever given her, searching for a sign that he *cared* about her for the same base, physical reasons most guys looked at her and wanted a piece.

"Yeah," he said. Then he quickly added a few words that he knew would stop her before she returned to the moment he'd first seen her in a bikini and admired the hell out of her *Sports Illustrated*-worthy body. "I'm also doing this because in my book it is always wrong to hit a woman. And I hope you'll change your mind about telling your dad, because Travis belongs behind bars for what he did to you."

She shook her head. "You're determined to be the hero, aren't you?"

"When it comes to your safety? Yeah, I'll play the part. You name the day, the time, the place—I'll be there to help you, Josie."

"Fine." She placed her hands on her hips and held her head high despite the red marks on her cheek and neck that clearly labeled her a victim. "The day? Today. The time? Right now. The place? Forever, Oregon. And your mission, Mr. White Knight? Drive me home and help me sneak back into my house."

Josie walked past him, her nose practically pointed to the clouds. The swing in her step drew his gaze to her perfect ass. He shouldn't look. But dammit, one glance and he didn't want to be the hero who snuck her back into her bedroom. He wanted to be the man who broke her out and showed her that relationships should never come with violence.

Chapter Two

FOREVER HATED HER with a vengeance. From the people
to the distant mountain range, everything about this
town seemed to be working against her. She was smart,
dammit. Heading to college on a full scholarship. And
still, this place was determined to land her in one mess
after another.

Josie stared out the window of Noah's pickup. The
main street faded into the distance as the truck sped
toward the college. Beyond the sprawling campus with
its odd mix of concrete structures and old brick buildings
stood her family home, empty apart from the dogs.

Except her dad's four-legged friends weren't supposed
to be alone. Her father had grounded her for breaking
curfew last weekend. And she'd ignored him because at
eighteen, she believed the time for "be home by midnight,
young lady" was behind her.

They drove past the edge of the campus and the landscape changed. Houses and barns dotted the rolling green hills. In a few weeks, she'd trade the wide-open space for Portland's downtown. She'd be free to set her own curfew. And free from boys who responded to a firm "it's over" by wrapping their hands around her neck.

She stole a glance at the man who'd sent her cowardly ex running away. Noah was living, breathing proof that fate refused to do her any favors. She could have handled Travis on her own. Her father was a police officer. Under her picture in her senior yearbook, it should have read "most likely to bring a man to his knees with a well-placed kick." Of course, her classmates had left off the kicking part when drafting the yearbook. And she'd ended up with "most likely to lose her underwear."

But the Forever High senior class's lack of faith in her abilities didn't change the fact that she could take on her ex-boyfriend. Travis might be a hundred pounds heavier, and armed with a supersized temper, but she'd learned self-defense from the best cops in the Willamette Valley.

She didn't need Noah's help. And pity? If he tried to "poor baby" her, she'd either burst into tears or jump out of the moving truck. Probably the latter. Because the thought of crying in front of the man who walked into her daydreams and declared, *Josephine Fairmore, I've loved you for years*—she would rather take her chances on the side of the road.

She stole another glance at Noah. He'd cut his blond hair short as if he wanted to show up ready to be one of The Few . . . The Brave . . . or whatever the marine motto was, the minute he arrived for basic training. And judging by the size of his look-at-me biceps, he'd also been lifting more than pint glasses behind his dad's bar.

She pressed her lips together, hating the visual reminder that he was leaving and might never come back. But Noah would be the perfect soldier. He'd carry honor, courage, and that too-perfect body onto the battlefield. As long as he survived, he'd come home a hero.

A man like Noah would never declare his undying love for his best friend's troublesome sister. No, he would run to her rescue in an alley and end their practically nonexistent relationship on the perfect note. On the bright and sunny side, he hadn't said the dreaded words—

"Josie, I have to ask." He slowed the truck as they approached her driveway. "Is this the first time?"

Hello, Mr. Rain Cloud.

They drove over the gravel in silence. But when they reached the parking area in front of her home, he threw the truck in park and turned to face her. "Please, Josie. Not knowing . . . it's killing me."

Killing *him*? As soon as she gave him an answer—truth or fiction—it would color the way he saw her. But after today that ship had probably set sail. She would always be someone who needed rescuing in his eyes. The victim. And wasn't that a great label to wear in front of the man of your dreams.

They're called dreams for a reason, aren't they? They're not supposed to come true.

"Once. And I dealt with it." She reached for the door.

He shook his head. "Travis didn't get the message."

"He's played football practically since he could walk.

After all those hits, it sometimes takes him a while to understand things." Her fingers froze on the door handle. "Not that all football players are stupid. I mean, you're not stupid."

And now the chances that you'll profess your undying love and steal a kiss before leaving are solidly lodged in never-going-to-happen land.

"I can be," he said, offering a half smile that quickly faded. "But I'd never hit a girl—or woman."

"And which one am I?" she challenged.

The corners of his lips turned up. It was amazing how easily his expression slipped into warm and welcoming mode. He'd been all doom and gloom when he'd rushed into the alley, but that wasn't Noah's default.

He upped the smile-wattage and gave her a full-blown grin. Was he aware of how inviting he appeared? His smile said *come closer and I'll show you . . .*

"How about we get you back into your bedroom so I can have a chat with Travis before work tonight?" He turned away from her and slid his superman-sized muscles out of the truck.

"I don't need your help," she said sharply as she slipped out of the passenger seat and slammed the truck door behind her. "I'm not your problem. Go home and work on your biceps."

His eyes widened as if referencing any part of his body crossed an imaginary line drawn in her dad's gravel driveway. Then he laughed and crossed his arms in front of his chest. "Is that what you think I do in my spare time?"

"Long days away from the bar at some mystery location . . ." She turned and headed for the back of the house. Her dad had taken her keys—house and car—when he'd grounded her, as if having a way back in and a vehicle were the only things keeping her from sneaking out. In a few weeks, she was heading to a school she'd fought her way into, one perfect grade at a time. She could find a way into town. And she knew how to phone a friend.

Of course, calling Travis for a ride and "conversation" didn't exactly highlight her intelligence.

"My brother thinks you're seeing someone," she added as they reached the back door.

"I'm not. Not that it's Dominic's business, or yours, but I've been taking my grandmother to the coast," he said, raising his right arm and placing his hand against the back of his neck. "She likes to see the ocean."

Wow. Could he stand any taller on the pedestal of perfection? He spent his downtime taking his eighty-something-year-old grandmother, who'd raised him alongside his dad, to the beach.

Perfect and single. She filed that fact away. Not that it mattered. They were both leaving soon. And she didn't plan on coming back to this town that seemed determined to ruin her.

"So how are you getting back in?" He lowered his arm and nodded to the house. "Need a boost in through a window?"

"Nah, I was using you for a ride. I left the back door to the kitchen unlocked and the dogs on guard." She climbed the steps to the wooden deck her father had built ten or so years ago with her big brother's help. Noah followed, avoiding the loose board no one had gotten around to fixing. He'd spent half his childhood and the years since his graduation at her house. Two guys, both raised by single dads who'd lost their wives suddenly—Noah's to a car crash, and hers and Dominic's to a sudden heart attack spurred by an underlying condition.

She'd been five when her mom died. And it had taken her a while to realize she wasn't going to follow a similar path. Her father had tried to explain it wasn't a genetic condition, but she'd been too young to comprehend how the person who'd cared for her around the clock just wasn't there anymore. By high school, she'd had a better understanding of genetics.

His brow furrowed. "Sure you're OK?"

No. Maybe. Yes? I'm just sad about the things I can't change. And how the ones I tried to fix turned out...

"I'll be fine." She turned the knob and opened the back door. "I'll see you around, Noah."

She stepped inside the white and blue farmhouse kitchen and closed the door. Forever's Golden Boy remained on the other side. She leaned against the solid wood, her hand still on the knob, and closed her eyes. Tears rolled down her cheeks. And she let herself feel . . . the lingering sting of Travis's palm against her face, the scratches around her neck.

Goddamn him!

She let out a sob. Just thinking about that moment— the panic, the need for a strength she didn't have—she never wanted to land in that place again. And if Noah hadn't rushed to her rescue . . .

She would still be standing in the alley, terrified. It was one thing to knee Travis in the balls, but she had a feeling it wouldn't have ended there. Discovery, Noah rushing to her rescue, had sent her now ex-boyfriend running. And even if her well-placed self-defense had pushed him away, it wouldn't change the fact that she'd placed herself in that situation. She'd snuck out of the house with that face-slapping ass. She'd planned to tell him it was over. But she should have known her boyfriend of almost a year wouldn't take it well. She'd witnessed his temper before.

So when it came to needing a rescue? That was on her.

"How did I land in this mess?" she whispered to the empty kitchen. But she already knew the answer. She hadn't been strong enough to turn her back on the promise of acceptance and popularity. If she dated the quarterback, if she stayed with Travis after half the town caught her in the back of the hay wagon, if she proved to everyone that they were "in love," not teenage lust, then maybe her family and everyone else in this town would see that she was more than a girl who made bad decisions. She could prove to everyone here that she was strong enough to endure the pointed looks and whispered comments.

But maybe, when it came to Forever, she should cut her losses and start fresh in Portland.

She raised her hands to her face and wiped away the tears. She would earn a degree in business management, start her own company, or take over someone else's and run it better. She'd find a man who liked what he saw when he looked at her. A man who offered kindness. And if he happened to be blond, with a warm smile, and perfect biceps . . .

No. Not Noah. She couldn't have him.

"Dominic would kill me, and Noah too," she muttered as she pushed off the door and headed for the stairs. Even if her brother's friend showed up on her doorstep and admitted he had a crush on her, he was still out of her reach—too perfect, too determined to do the right thing.

Chapter Three

July 2012

Noah raised his Smith & Wesson and waited for the range safety officer to give the all clear. He stared at the target in the distance. Ten shots. He could place every one in the center. But he didn't want to shoot at a damn piece of paper. He wished like hell he could fire holes through his reasons for leaving Forever.

With one well-placed bullet, he wanted to blow away his family's financial problems. And yeah, he'd put a hole through his dad's reasons to keep Big Buck's a country western bar.

For two generations loggers have visited this bar. They come here after a long, shitty day and pretend they have

what it takes to be a cowboy. For eight seconds after work,
these guys are stars.

Except more and more had been landing on their
asses before the buzzer. And they hadn't come back for
more. There were too many "kids" from the university
in the area. Housing prices had gone up and the loggers
had moved to Independence Falls and some of the other
neighboring towns.

Noah knew they'd make more if they took out the
mechanical bull and changed the place into a nightclub.
Sure, the remaining locals who kept Forever's Main Street
looking like a picture-perfect, all-American town might
protest. But the students would flock to the place. And
the twenty-something university crowd didn't sit at the
bar nursing one beer all night. They drank mixed drinks
and shots.

"Fire!" the volunteer safety officer called.

He pressed the trigger. Once. Twice. The bullets spi-
raled to the target. In a few weeks, maybe months, he
wouldn't be shooting at stationary pieces of paper. If he
deployed . . .

Shit. He lowered his weapon. Not if. *When* he deployed to one of the countries no one in their right mind
put on their list of dream vacation spots, he'd shoot to
defend, to protect, and to kill.

Noah set his gun on the table. He moved through the
motions, releasing the clip, racking the slide, and eject-
ing the round from the chamber. He set the piece and the
ammunition down. Then he stepped back from the line,

vaguely aware of the people moving around him. The range safety officer had called out "cease fire" and he'd been so caught up in the future, the what might happen when he left, that he'd missed it.

He stared down the range and out into the rolling hills lined with evergreens. *So damn beautiful.* He wished he could stay in the Willamette Valley, surrounded by the familiar scenery and the people he loved. But someone needed to make enough to pay for his grandmother's retirement. And her rising medical costs.

"Noah!" a familiar voice barked.

He turned away from the hills in the distance and focused on the two men standing just beyond the line in his bay.

"Take off your ears," Dominic hollered, raising his right hand to his ear.

Noah pulled off the safety gear that blocked out a helluva lot, including Josie's brother.

"Hey," Noah said, nodding to the man who was unmistakably related to Josie. He had the same dark hair and green eyes. Although the similarities stopped there. Dominic had played center for the Forever football team. He was built like a tank and stood an inch or two taller than Noah. He was going to make one helluva soldier. Plus, Josie's brother had been itching to enlist since graduation. His father had tried to steer him toward the police academy, but after a few years of working with his dad, Dominic wanted more of a challenge.

And Noah wanted to stay right here and shoot at fucking paper.

"You didn't hear a word we said, did you?" Ryan smiled, looking more like a movie star type than a football hero—probably because he'd rarely taken the field as the backup kicker. And Ryan sure as shit didn't look like a future air force pilot.

Noah forced a grin. "Had my ears on."

"I said I bet Travis is glad you went after him with your fists," Dominic informed him. "Not your pistol."

"Yeah." Noah shoved his hands in his pockets, his knuckles still raw from sparring with Travis Taylor. He'd had the upper hand. He'd approached the kid angry and knowing he planned to land a hit or two. Sure, he'd waited two weeks, giving Josie's face time to heal so that no one would connect the pieces.

"Any reason you hit my sister's boyfriend?" Dominic asked mildly.

"Ex-boyfriend," Noah corrected. He turned to the table to pick up his gear.

Dominic held out a hand to help. "They've broken up before and gotten back together."

"They won't this time." Noah shook his head, declining his friend's helping hand, and headed for the viewing gallery.

"Why?" Dominic demanded, abandoning his easygoing tone. "What the fuck happened?"

"Ask your sister," Noah said. "But our fight—"

"That wasn't a fight," Ryan jumped in once they were alone in the small room designed for spectators. A bulletproof glass window separated the space from the range where the other shooters were heading back to the line.

"You took Travis out, man," Ryan continued. "At least that's what I heard."

"He pissed me off." Noah shrugged and headed for the gun case he'd stashed in the corner with his duffel. "And it wasn't all about Josie."

I wanted to make sure the kid thinks twice before hurting another woman. I wanted Travis to remember how his damn nose felt when I landed that hit.

"Some kid pisses you off and you swing?" Dominic said from behind him. "Why didn't you drive your temper over here, to the shooting range?"

"I did," he admitted, closing his case. *Afterward.* He picked up his stuff and turned around, ready to get the hell away from here.

"She won't tell me anything," Dominic said, and he moved closer, blocking Noah's path to the door.

Noah stared at his friend and saw the same determination that had radiated from Josie the other night. "Look, it's not my story to tell. But I'll say this. That asshole Travis doesn't deserve her and he won't go near her again."

His best friend since damn near forever stared back at him as if waiting for Noah to crack and spill more about what had led to Travis Taylor's broken nose.

Noah just held his gaze.

Finally, Dominic took a step back. "Thanks for looking out for her. I wish you'd tell me what went down . . ."

Noah shook his head.

"But," Dominic continued, his face breaking into a rare smile, "as long as you're taking on the big brother role—"

"I'm not . . ." But he couldn't finish the sentence. Because when it came to Josie, he wasn't about to tell Dominic he'd ever considered another role.

"Hey, now." His friend held up his hands. "You're not encroaching. I've looked out for her crazy ass long enough. You're welcome to take a turn. Though I should warn you that if you break any more noses my dad might get suspicious. I'm not part of the force anymore, so I can't bring you in for questioning and all."

"I'm not going to start another fight." Noah tried to move toward the door, but Dominic sidestepped and blocked his path.

"Where are you heading in such a hurry?" Dominic asked. He wasn't threatening now, he was teasing. "Beach date with your grandmother?"

Ryan laughed and Noah shook his head. "So Josie told you that much, huh?"

"Yeah," his friend said. "And I figured that as long as you were feeling like a big brother and all, you could take Josie with you."

"What?" There was no way in hell he wanted to spend an hour in a car with his gran and a woman—yeah, he considered Josie all woman now—who defined indecent thoughts. What would they talk about? The time Gran tried to potty train him and he'd peed all over the house? That was her favorite embarrassing childhood tale. Or maybe how he'd saved Josie from her abusive boyfriend?

"My dad's working today, but I'm free. And Lily's done teaching for the summer so we thought we'd spend the afternoon together, seeing as I'm leaving soon and all."

"You want Josie out of the house so you and your girlfriend can make some noise," Noah said, filling in the blanks. "Why don't you just ask her to leave?"

"She's still grounded," Ryan supplied. And judging from his grin, he found it pretty damn funny that Noah was getting stuck with watching wild, little Josie Fairmore.

Only she wasn't little anymore. And he wasn't sure the "wild" label fit either. Not in a break-all-the-rules context. But maybe . . .

Don't go there.

"She begged to come to the going away party tomorrow night at your place," Dominic explained. "Dad refused the first dozen or so times she asked, seeing as there will be alcohol served. He's a stickler about the legal age thing. Then he changed his mind. As long as I keep an eye on her. At the party and every minute leading up to it."

"You agreed to babysit?" Noah asked.

"She's eighteen," Dominic said. "She doesn't need a babysitter. But if she gets into trouble, she can't come to the party. I don't want her sitting at home alone on my last night in town."

"Take Lily someplace else," Noah said. "Problem solved."

Dominic shook his head. "Her mom is retired and home all the time. And you know her parents don't want her to move out and get her own place until she's freaking married."

"Fine." They only had forty-eight hours until they reported for basic training. And he knew they all wanted to make the most of their time. "But why doesn't Ryan take Josie?"

"I promised Helena I'd give her a hand with her farm chores so we can grab a bite tonight," Ryan said. The next, great air force pilot was tight with him and Dom, but Helena was his closest friend in Forever. They'd never crossed the line into naked friends—and probably never would—but she likely topped the list of people Ryan would think about while he learned to fly fighter jets.

Noah looked at Dominic. "Tell Josie I'll pick her up in an hour."

And remember you asked for this.

JOSIE SLIPPED OFF her sneakers and sank her toes in the sand. Sandals would have been a better choice, but Dominic hadn't given her much time to get ready. He'd stormed into the house, told her she was going to the coast for the afternoon, and if she tried to stay he'd tell Dad not to let her go to the party. She'd run to change out of her sweats and into jean shorts, a V-neck T-shirt, and the first shoes she could find.

"I've always loved the feel of sand between my toes," Noah's grandmother said as she settled into the beach chair he'd set out for her. "Noah thinks I come for the chowder, but I just like to hear the sound of the ocean and feel the sand between my toes."

"You've got it wrong, Gran." Noah lowered to one knee beside his grandmother's feet. He gently lifted one foot and slipped off her orthopedic shoe and then the other.

"I drive out here for the chowder. The ocean and the company are a bonus."

His grandmother laughed, then leaned her head back and closed her eyes. "Why don't you two take a walk, enjoy the beach, while I rest and listen to the waves?"

Noah stood. "We'll be nearby."

"Don't stay too close," she muttered to her grandson, eyes still closed. "I'm serious about my nap."

"I know," Noah said, shaking his head. "I know."

Leaving her shoes near the beach chair, Josie headed for the packed sand by the water. The tides were out and the beach was quiet for a Friday afternoon. Noah moved to her side and easily matched her pace.

"I should probably thank you for breaking Travis's nose, but—"

"You're welcome."

She glanced up from the sand and caught him smiling. "*But,* I wish I'd been able to do it myself."

"I like playing the hero, Josie," he said, placing a hand on her elbow and guiding her up the beach, away from the wave rushing in.

So much for low tide and taking care of myself.

"Is that why you're joining the marines?" she asked.

"No." He stopped and turned to look out at the ocean.

"Then why go? I know Dominic has been thinking about it for a while. Have you?"

He glanced in his grandmother's direction. "We're out of earshot. Want to sit down?"

No, she didn't want sand in her shorts. But she wasn't going to pass up a chance to sit next to Noah and stare out at the waves. What were the odds she'd ever find herself alone with him again in a place like this? It was like a scene in a romantic movie—except for the sleeping grandmother.

She settled onto the ground, burying her toes in the sand again. Her arms wrapped around her legs.

"With the marines, I'll get a guaranteed paycheck and benefits," he said, lowering onto the beach beside her.

"You could find that here. I mean, you have a job at your dad's bar."

"Big Buck's Country Bar isn't making enough to support three people," he said. "It might turn around now that I've convinced my dad to take out the mechanical bull. But a new sound system would help. Some DJs. A bigger dance floor."

"Wait, you took out the bull? I never had a chance to ride it."

"It's in my barn if you want to try it out," he said with a laugh. "Dad set it up as if people might come out and visit the damn thing."

"They might." *I might if you'll watch me ride it.*

But she wasn't exactly cowgirl material. She'd never owned farm animals. Still, she had the boots in her closet . . .

"They're welcome to the bull as long as it stays in the barn." He looked down at the sand. "I'm planning to send home as much of my paycheck as I can spare. That should help with my grandmother's expenses and cover the new sound system."

"That's sweet," she murmured.

"It's reality," he said. "I can make more and hopefully do some good."

"Are you scared?" The question slipped out. "Sorry. I've been watching Dominic and wondering . . . but he doesn't act afraid."

"I'm not sure he is." He drew circles in the sand with his toes, not looking up at her. "But yeah, I'm scared. There are aspects of fighting, going out there with a loaded weapon . . ."

"You're a great shot." That fact gave her some comfort.

"Yeah, but this will be different." He looked up at her, his expression open, honest, and so vulnerable it made her heart ache.

"I don't want to let my team, the guys I'm serving with—I don't want to let them down," he continued. "Not out there, in places where it counts a helluva lot more than on the football field."

"You won't." And oh God, she wanted to wrap her arms around his supersized muscles and hold him tight.

"I hope you're right."

"I am." She reached out and placed her hand on his arm. "I mean, listen to yourself. Even your fears are perfect."

"I'm not perfect, Josie." His voice had shifted, the sound low, rough, and so unlike him. "If I was . . . shit."

He stared at her hand and then lifted his gaze to her lips. And she silently prayed her facial expression didn't scream *please, please, please, do it! Kiss me!*

But then he looked away and pulled his arm free from

her touch. He stood and held out his hand to help her up. "We should get back."

But she didn't trust herself to touch him. Not when she still wanted a Noah Tager kiss more than anything this world had to offer her.

He lowered his outstretched arm as she pushed herself off the sand, dusting off her butt. There was sand in her shorts. But it had been worth it.

"I don't want your brother thinking I kept you out too long," he said. "He might make it difficult for you to go to the party."

"I'll be there," she said firmly. *Even if I have to sneak out of the house again.*

"Good." He turned and started walking toward his grandmother's beach chair. "Because I'd like to see you ride that bull before I go."

Chapter Four

ONE MORE NIGHT. Don't waste it.

Noah stared into the flames. With Dominic and Ryan's help, he'd built one helluva campfire on his dad's land, not far from the barn. Pickups formed a barrier on one side. Their tailgates were parked a safe distance from the flames. But they remained close enough for couples and groups of people he'd known his entire life to huddle together. The keg stood opposite the lines of trucks on the other side of the fire. And behind it, the woods he'd played in as a kid.

One more night. He wanted to enjoy it—right or wrong. Because he wasn't going to come home the same. He knew it. And it scared the hell out of him.

He scanned the crowd. Dominic was holding court, his legs dangling over the back of his dad's truck and his arm around Lily. He couldn't find Ryan. But he'd spotted him earlier, heading to the house with Helena. They'd been on a mission to raid his dad's liquor cabinet. Knowing his father wouldn't mind, Noah had given them the go-ahead.

One more night. And he wanted Josie Fairmore—the only person in Forever who'd asked, *Are you scared?*

He spotted her, standing off to the side of the keg with a red plastic cup in her hand. Her white sundress glowed in the firelight, hugging her curves and offering a stellar view of her legs. She wore her dark hair long and loose around her shoulders. And a pair of brown leather cowboy boots on her feet.

Noah was by her side before he realized he'd been walking, dodging backslaps from old friends. Sure, he'd smiled at them, but he'd wanted to get to Josie.

"Your dad would probably ground you for the rest of the year if he saw you sipping on that." He nodded to the cup poised at her lips.

She lowered her drink. "Trying to save me from my dad now?"

"No."

Tonight I want to land you in trouble. The kind that will piss off your dad and your brother. But it doesn't have a damn thing to do with drinking.

"Well, it's water. I haven't touched the beer tonight." She lifted her free hand and ran her index finger around the rim of her cup. "And I'm leaving for college in a few weeks. I doubt my father will bother driving up to Portland to ground me."

"Would you listen if he did?"

"Probably not."

"So . . ." Shit, he was acting like he'd never spoken to a woman before. And this was Josie.

Because it was Josie, he had to ask. "Has Travis left you alone?"

She nodded and her smiled faded. "He hasn't called, texted, or emailed. And I don't miss him."

"Glad you're not heartbroken." *Because I'm dying to take you into the barn and watch you ride that damn bull in your little, white dress.*

"Not even close. I'm more upset about the fact that you're leaving tomorrow. Not just you, I mean. Dominic too."

She turned her gaze to the grass at her feet. It was green, which was unusual for this time of year. The fact that they'd had some rain and were still free and clear from forest fire danger had allowed them to build the bonfire.

"Nice boots," he said, ready to slam the door on words like "Travis" and "leaving."

She lifted her chin. And the look in her green eyes? It spelled mischief. "You mentioned something about riding . . ."

"The bull." He nodded to the barn. "It's in there. Follow me." *And make my fantasy come true.*

He was one beer into the night, so he knew it wasn't alcohol driving him. He wanted Josie. On the bull, on the cushions surrounding the machine—it didn't matter as long as she was in his arms.

"Sure there won't be a line?" she asked, walking at his side through the darkness to the mostly empty pole barn that at one time, when his grandfather was alive, had housed cows, goats, and even a llama.

He shook his head. "I locked it up for the night. I didn't want a bunch of drunken idiots taking rides and getting hurt. Plus, my dad would be pissed if someone broke it."

"You'll start it off slow so I won't get hurt?" she asked, her voice low.

"Yeah," he said, withdrawing the key from his jeans and slipping it into the locked side door. But he wasn't sure they were talking about the bull anymore.

He led the way inside and flipped the light switch. The fluorescent strips overhead illuminated a dusty dirt floor. His grandfather had talked about pouring concrete one day, but they'd never had the money. A collection of boxes and old furniture stood at the far end. The black bull stood in the center of a padded section that filled one corner of the barn. At one point in time, the pads had been red, white, and blue, but they'd faded, losing their all-American look.

"It has horns." Josie moved past him and stepped up onto a firm greyish-white cushion. "And a face."

"That's real cowhide," he said, keeping his boots planted in the dirt. If he joined her up there, he'd reach for her. And he wanted to see her ride first. His dick was hard at the thought. Having a hard-on around Josie should have sent him running toward a cold shower. But not tonight.

One more night. . .

He watched as she ran her hand over the black hide, down the bull's neck to the leather strap that ran down the machine's side. At the base of the bull's neck, the strap connected to a handle. Some of the fancy models included a mock saddle. But Big Buck's bull looked like the real deal. His dad used to brag that this was what cowboys used for training.

She placed one hand on the handle and the other on the smooth surface covering the machine's back. Glancing over her shoulder, she raised an eyebrow. "Can I take it for a ride now?"

Oh hell yeah.

"Sure." He headed for the controls, keeping an eye on Josie. She gripped the handle and pulled herself up. It wasn't a graceful mounting, not even close. But the way her sundress rode up her legs, flashing her white cotton panties beneath—he was eight seconds away from pulling her off the damn thing before he hit go.

Turning away, he focused on the controls. He set the speed to slow and then called, "Ready?"

"Think so," she said. "Does this look like a good position?"

He looked up and let out a low groan. Her bare legs held tight to the cowhide, leaving her dress bunched around her hips. And she gripped the handle with both hands. "Yeah," he managed as he hit the big green button. "You're good."

The machine hummed to life, sounding nothing like the animals the real cowboys risked life and limb to ride. Slowly, it began to pitch forward and back, all the while spinning in a gentle circle. It looked like a bull on tranquilizers—or a machine designed to seduce.

Josie slid down to the neck. She took one hand off the handle and reached for the horns. Her upper body pitched forward. The machine tipped back and her panty-covered bottom glided a few inches in the other direction.

"Hold on tight with your legs," he called. "And move your upper body against the movement."

"Huh?" She pitched forward again, but this time, she fought to lean back. A few more turns and her body would find the motion.

But helping her wouldn't hurt . . .

Noah climbed up onto the padding. "Would you like a lesson?"

"You're going to climb on while this thing is moving?" she said without looking at him. She was focused on her grip and the bull.

He laughed. "It's not going that fast, sweetheart." The pet name slipped out and he saw her eyes widen. But that could have been due to the bull's motion. "And I've had a lot of practice on this thing," he added.

"Show me," she demanded. There was a breathless quality to her usually defiant tone.

He waited until the side of the bull faced him. Then, he reached for the handle, covering her hand with his, and scrambled on. She fell forward and he probably looked like an ass while he worked to get his leg around the moving machine, but a few seconds later he was settled. His hips pressed up against her backside as the bull's head reared into the air.

"Lean back," he said, wrapping one arm around her waist. His other hand maintained a hold on the handle beside her white-knuckled grip. "And relax. I've got you. The worst that can happen is you fall on your ass."

"I'd rather keep my ass and my pride off the ground," she murmured, letting her back rest against his chest.

Holding her close, he guided their bodies, pitching them toward the bull's head when the rear end lowered. He leaned back when it kicked up as if lifting its nonexistent hind legs in the air.

"You would be one helluva of a sight at a rodeo," he murmured.

"Because I didn't think to wear jeans?" she teased, sounding a lot more relaxed now that they'd found a rhythm.

"I like your dress, Josie." His gaze fixed on the back of her neck. Her hair had fallen forward, over her shoulders, during the first few moves. And now her neck was exposed.

So damn tempting.

"I thought the boots were a good fit," she said, talking as if she needed to fill the silence. "For my debut as a cowgirl."

"You look like one right now."

She rocked back against him. By now, she had to be aware of his dick, hard and begging for action beneath his fly. What the hell was he waiting for? He had the woman he'd dreamed about, knowing he shouldn't touch her, in his arms.

One more night. You have one more chance before everything changes.

"I'm going to kiss you." Not wanting to let go of her or

the strap, he lowered his lips to the nape of her neck. He touched her skin, one brief, soft tease. "Here."

"On the bull," she said as she leaned into him and wiggled her hips.

No way in hell she missed how much I want her.

The bull's head dropped and he pressed his mouth against her neck, kissing, licking, exploring . . .

She turned her head and offered her lips, her green eyes wide. One look confirmed that she wanted this. Probably not as much as he did, but he'd bet she hadn't been daydreaming about him in a swimsuit.

"Josie," he murmured. His fingers wrapped around her slim waist, holding on tight. His mouth touched hers. Eight seconds into the kiss that threatened to break his restraint—he wanted her, now, on the back of a damn bull—her lips parted and she kissed him back, taking their somewhat innocent lip-lock straight into hot and heavy.

She broke away, but his attention, every cell in his body, remained focused on her.

"Have you ever ridden the bull naked?" she asked.

"No." But her low voice made the sound of cowhide against bare butt seem like a brilliant idea.

"Hmm," she murmured, glancing down. "Place your hand on my thigh."

He released his hold on her waist and followed her instructions. Her skin felt so damn good beneath his palm. He inched upward. "For a better grip."

"You're going to need it," she said. "I'm letting go."

A second later, both of her hands were reaching for

the bottom of the material bunched around her hips. Holding tight with his thighs, he withdrew his right hand from the handle and placed it on her other leg.

She pulled her dress over her head and tossed it forward. One of the thin shoulder straps caught on the bull's right horn. The dress hung there, spinning around.

"Looks like the bull's waving the white flag," she said. *Sweetheart, I'm ready and willing to surrender.*

"Lose the bra, Josie," he said gruffly. "Let's take this naked bull ride all the way."

But she didn't reach for the back clasp. Instead, she slipped her hand in the handle and looked over her shoulder at him.

"You're sure?" she said softly.

"I want you." And yeah, he supposed he'd known that he would need to toss that fact out there tonight alongside a few others. "I have for a while. I've respected your brother, steering clear, but I want to spend the last few hours before I go with *you.*"

"Noah—" Her eyes widened as if she hadn't expected this speech.

But he wasn't done yet. "You can pull your dress back on and we can just sit here, watch the bull spin, and talk until the sun comes up. But I'd rather take that naked ride."

She let go and leaned forward, her fingers deftly working to strip off her bra. "Don't let me fall."

"I won't." He slid his hands up her thighs, over her white underwear to her waist while she tossed her bra to the mat.

"Ah hell, Josie, I want to turn you around and bury

my face in your breasts," he said. And yeah, he heard the raw desire in his voice. "I want to claim every damn inch of you."

His hands moved higher, brushing the underside of her breast. He couldn't resist. He had to touch her. Cupping one full breast in each hand, he ran his fingers over her nipples, offering gentle squeezes. She gasped and leaned back, her hips moving with the bull's rhythm.

"I want to taste you, touch you, fuck you right here," he growled. "I want you so damn much. But—" He had to tell her. He needed to make it clear. "But I'm still leaving in the morning. Nothing will change that."

JOSIE FELT REALITY rush in, fighting for space alongside the tantalizing feeling of Noah's hands on her breasts, his lips on her neck, his body pressed against hers. And this bull—the hum and gentle vibration beneath them threatened to push her over the edge. Until he said those words.

I'm still leaving in the morning. Nothing will change that.

"I know," she said simply.

His hands stilled, no longer tracing circles and exploring her nipples. *Oh no, he's walking away. He's heading for the honorable path.*

"Is it possible?" she asked, needing to keep him here, mounted on this spinning, bucking machine. "To turn around and face you for the rest of our naked ride?"

He chuckled. "I don't know. Might depend on how flexible you are."

"I don't think that's our problem," she murmured. Although that might be a little white lie. She wasn't Gumby. Not even close. "But you still have your clothes on."

He released her and she felt his hand moving behind her. A second later, his shirt landed on the faded red section of the surrounding mat. "I can't get my jeans off on this thing," he said.

"How about I turn around and release your zipper?" She drew one knee up and froze. "I might need some help," she added.

His hands returned to her waist. "Can you move your leg over the head the next time it dips forward? I've got you."

She nodded, trusting in his hold. The bull reared and she swung her left leg over the top and . . . slid right off the other side. She landed on her hands and knees.

"Shit," he cursed. And then he was beside her, wrapping his arms around her and pulling her away from the faded blue into the not-so-pure white area. "Before it swings back around," he added.

She ended up on top of him, her bare chest against his superman-sized muscles. "Sorry. I just really wanted to get you out of your pants," she said, looking down at him.

"Done." He gently shifted her onto the mat beside him and reached for the button. She sat up and watched as he stripped off his jeans and boxers. He kicked them aside and unveiled his long, thick cock.

"I want to take you for a ride," she said, unable to keep a healthy dose of "oh wow" from her voice. She'd only been with one man before. And even though he'd played football like Noah, he'd clearly been an inch or two shorter on all counts.

"Josie." He weaved his fingers through her hair, curled his upper body up off the mat, and crushed his mouth to hers. There was nothing tentative about his kiss this time. He was taking her, claiming her, demanding everything she had to give.

His other hand slipped beneath her panties, touching her, exploring her.

"Help me get them off," she murmured, pulling back from his kiss. "My underwear."

"There's no rush. We can take our time," he said, but he helped draw her panties down as she brought her legs closer, one knee on either side of his thigh.

With a few more wiggles and kicks, she won the battle with her panties. She stared down at the amused man beneath her. Noah. The man of her dreams. The guy who always smiled. But this time it was for *her*.

She shifted back. Her bare ass rested on his thigh and she wrapped her hand around his cock. She placed her other hand on his abs. "Do you know what it feels like to have a giant machine rocking beneath you, vibrating just a touch but not enough to do more than tease?"

He let out a low laugh, his eyes darting between her face and her hand, now moving up and down the smooth skin of his erection. She kept her touch light. She didn't want him to come like this.

"When what you really want, what you've wanted for so damn long, is sitting right behind you?" There, she'd said it. She'd admitted that she'd wanted him too. "And knowing that you only have a few hours before the man you never thought would ever take you on a naked bull ride leaves?"

His smile faded and he reached his hand up to cup her face. "I know, Josie. Not about the vibrating, but about the wanting."

"I'm not waiting, Noah." She kept her hand wrapped around his cock as she lifted her hips off his leg. She moved forward until she was poised over him, ready to sink onto his oh-wow length. She sank down, feeling him stretch her open, filling her up.

"Jesus, Josie," he hissed. Then he grabbed her hips and tried to lift her off. "We need a condom."

"Just pull out," she said, claiming another inch. She'd expected discomfort, something other than this I-might-come-before-my-clit-even-rubs-against-him feeling. And that had never happened before. "Plus—"

"I can't risk it. I'm leaving," he said through clenched teeth.

"—I'm on the pill." She rocked her hips back and forth as she'd done on the bull, lifting an inch and feeling him slide out before lowering back down.

"You're sure?" he gasped, his hands holding tight, but no longer trying to stop her.

"Please, Noah, take me for a ride."

Chapter Five

I'M GOING TO picture her breasts every damn time I close my eyes.

Noah couldn't take his eyes off Josie as she placed her hands flat on his chest, arched her lower back, and began to ride him. Her breasts swung forward and he took it as an invitation. Curling his abs, he caught one sweet, tempting nipple with his mouth and began to suck.

"Oh God, Noah," she called above him, her words drowning out the sound of the bull still spinning and bucking beside them. Her hips ground into him in earnest—searching, needing, wanting . . .

Sweetheart, I'm going to give you a ride you won't forget.

He rocked his hips up and off the mat, driving into her. He released her breast, but quickly replaced his lips with his hands. He wanted to see her, watch her face while she came. And he sure as hell wanted to remember this moment.

"Noah. Oh, Noah," she screamed. His named echoed in the barn as she moved faster and faster, taking him with her. He was so damn close . . . But he couldn't, not yet. She had to come first. She had to—

"Noah!"

Her body gripped him, convulsing around him as her hips slowed their needy, desperate motions.

"Noah," she said, her voice shifting from a scream to a near whisper. But she kept her head thrown back, her eyes closed. "Oh God, Noah. I love you."

No. She couldn't.

"Don't say that, Josie." Agony rose up to great the pleasure radiating from his very happy dick. But the pleasure won. "Oh fuck . . . you can't . . ."

He couldn't hold back. He thrust up into her and gave in to the blinding, mind-numbing sensations, the pure contentment that took hold, making the rest of the world fade away for one beautiful, perfect moment.

And then it came rushing back. Josie Fairmore had said "I love you" while he had his dick buried in her.

He opened his eyes and looked up at her. God, he'd rip out his heart and hand it to her if he could. But he was leaving. And the place he was going, where they would train him to shoot at people instead of paper, to rush into a war he didn't fully understand—he couldn't take her heart there.

He needed to say something, to leave her with something. But what could he say to the beautiful woman looking down at him as if her orgasm had sent her tumbling into a pit of sadness?

"I'm sorry," she whispered.

"Don't be. Josie, I'm the one who should apologize. I'm the one . . ."

Who wants to love you, but can't.

"Noah?" A fist pounded on the side door. "Noah, are you in there?" His best friend's voice called through the door.

Shit, I hope I locked it.

"Hold on. I'm here," he called before Dominic tested the handle.

Josie's eyes widened, but she didn't move.

"Sweetheart," he murmured. "I'm sorry." And yeah, it was becoming clear it was one of many apologies he owed her. He'd wanted to be the one who made sure no one ever hurt her again. Her hero. Not the man who broke her heart. But playing the hero had slipped out of reach this time, beyond his control.

"I need to go," he said. "I think I locked the door, but—"

"That won't keep Dom out." She raised her hips, letting his semi-hard dick slip out as she moved to the mat.

"Yeah." He got to his feet and started pulling on his clothes. But she didn't move. "Josie?" he asked, slipping his feet into his shoes.

"I just need a minute," she said softly, wrapping her arms around her naked legs.

"What are you doing in there?" Dominic called. "Riding that bull alone?"

"What makes you think he's alone?" Ryan said dryly.

Ah hell.

Noah stepped off the mat. "I'm sorry, Josie," he murmured, hoping Dominic wouldn't overhear.

She just stared back at him. "Goodbye, Noah."

He heard the knob rattle. He'd locked it. But still, Dominic wasn't stupid. If he'd realized Josie was missing from the party too . . .

"Don't break the damn thing," Noah called as he opened it. He stepped out into the night, forcing his friends to move back. He quickly pulled the door closed behind him.

"What's up?" he asked.

"The party's dying down," Ryan said. His friend wasn't smiling and hell, he looked as if he'd gotten into it with someone. His button-down flannel was untucked from his jeans, and he was off by a button.

And yeah, Noah was too busy wondering what had happened to Ryan to see it coming.

At the last second, he saw a flash of skin near his face. A fist. And then pain shot through his jaw. He reeled back, lost his footing, and landed on his ass in the dirt outside the barn door.

"Zip up your damn fly," Dominic growled, lowering his fist.

Shit. He deserved that hit. Maybe another one for the way he'd left Josie naked and in fu¢king love with him beside the damn bull.

Noah slowly got to his feet, stepped back out of Dominic's reach, and zipped up his fly.

"I'm not stupid," Dominic said as he turned and headed back to the fire. "Josie's been missing from the party for a while."

"I know. But you should know . . . I care about her," he said, following him, Ryan falling in at his side.

But I can't love her. . .

Dominic kept walking toward the bonfire, Lily, and the circle of friends determined to send them off on a high note.

"Doesn't change the fact that you're leaving," Dominic said flatly.

"No." Noah glanced back at the barn. He should go back in there. He should turn off the damn bull and help her find her dress. And then what? Tell her he was sorry again? He was leaving tomorrow and he might never come back. He couldn't offer promises because he damn sure couldn't keep them. "You're right, it doesn't change a thing."

Except Josie.

Yeah, he had a feeling the hurt he'd left behind had cut deep. And he didn't have a clue how to make that right.

That was on him. But he hoped like hell the pain would fade. She'd find someone else, a man who wasn't heading for a war zone.

Noah closed his eyes. *If the next guy hurts her. . .*

"One more drink," Dominic said. "And then that's it. The party is over. Time to head home and prepare to leave in the morning."

JOSIE WATCHED THE bull spin in slow circles. Her discarded dress waved through the air like a bright white flag. She hadn't planned for her clothes to end up riding the machine without her. She'd walked into the barn hoping for a kiss, maybe a little more.

But she hadn't planned on this. She'd never in a million years wish for this ending.

"He left," she whispered as she sat up. But even if her words had been audible over the constant mechanical hum, there was no one here. He'd walked away.

And yes, her brother had knocked. It was either be caught naked together or find a way to keep Dominic out. She understood that. But when he'd rushed to gather his clothes, mumbling apologies, she'd felt the wound open up. He'd taken a piece of her with him. And she had a horrible feeling it was her heart.

"That's going to leave a scar," she told the bull as she pushed off the mat and headed for the controls. She hit the red stop button and then climbed onto the red section to reclaim her clothes.

I'm strong enough to put it behind me. Bury the pain and move forward. I've done it before and I'll do it again.

But that wouldn't erase the scar.

Give in to your Impulses . . .
Continue reading for excerpts from
our newest Avon Impulse books.
Available now wherever e-books are sold.

HARD EVER AFTER
A HARD INK NOVELLA
By Laura Kaye

WILD AT HEART
By T.J. Kline

THE BRIDE WORE STARLIGHT
A SEVEN BRIDES FOR SEVEN COWBOYS NOVEL
By Lizbeth Selvig

An Excerpt from

HARD EVER AFTER
A Hard Ink Novella
By Laura Kaye

After a long battle to discover the truth, the men
and women of Hard Ink have a lot to celebrate,
especially the wedding of two of their own—
Nick Rixey and Becca Merritt—whose hard-
fought love deserves a happy ending. As Nick and
the team shift from crisis mode to building their
new security consulting firm, Becca heads back to
work at the ER. But amid the everyday chaos of
their demanding jobs and upcoming nuptials, an
old menace they thought was long gone reemerges,
threatening the peace they've only just found.

Wearing only her bra and jeans, Becca sat in a chair in the middle of Nick's tattoo room. Since the shop was closed while Jeremy focused on getting the construction on the other half of the building started, they were the only ones down there. The driving beat of a rock song played from the radio as Nick moved around the room getting everything ready.

Cabinets and a long counter filled one wall, which was otherwise decorated with drawings, tattoo designs, posters, and photographs of clients.

Becca had seen Nick work before and loved the dichotomy of this hard-edged, lethal soldier having a soft, artistic side. He was really freaking talented, too.

He handed her three sheets of paper. "I worked up a couple different fonts. What do you think?"

She shifted between the pages. "This one," she said, settling on the cursive design that best interweaved the letters in the words *Only, Always, Forever.*

"That was my favorite, too," he said, giving her a wink. "How is this for size? Bigger? Smaller?"

The total design as he had it on the sheet was about four inches square, the words stacked atop one another. "This looks good to me. What do you think?"

Nick nodded and came behind her. He folded the sheet to focus on the design, then held it against the back of her right shoulder. "Yeah. This is a good size for the space. Gonna be fucking beautiful." He leaned down and pressed a kiss to her skin. "Let me go make the stencil, and we're ready to go."

A few minutes later, he cleaned her skin, affixed the stencil, and let her look at its placement before getting her settled into the chair again.

He pulled her bra strap off to the side. "Ready?"

"Very," she said, butterflies doing a small loop in her belly.

The tattoo machine came to life on a low buzz. "Just relax and let me know if you need a break, okay?" he said, dipping the tip into a little plastic cup of black ink.

"Okay." His gloved hands fell against her skin, and then the needles. Almost a scratching feeling, it didn't hurt nearly as bad as she thought it would. And just like when he'd drawn on her with skin markers, she was already dying to see what it looked like.

"How you doing?" he asked in a voice full of concentration she found utterly sexy. Just the thought that he was permanently altering her skin—just like he'd permanently altered her heart, her life, her very soul—sent a hot thrill through her blood.

"I'm good," she said, relaxing into the sensation of the bite moving across her skin. "Is it weird that I kinda like how it feels?"

He didn't answer right away as the needle moved in a long line. He pulled the machine away and wiped at her shoulder. "Not weird at all," he said, his voice a little gravelly. "Some people like the sensation and even find getting tattoos addictive."

"I can see that," she said. He worked without talking for a stretch, and the combination of the quiet intensity radiating off of him, the driving rock beat, and the buzz of the machine was heady and intoxicating. She found herself breathing a little faster and wanting so much more of him to be touching so much more of her. If she thought he was sexy putting ink on someone else, it was nothing compared to how she felt when he was doing it to her.

"What are you thinking about so hard?" Nick asked, his breath caressing her bare shoulder.

"Really want to know?" she asked, already smiling at what his reaction might be.

"Always," he said, wiping at her skin. He dipped the machine in the ink and leaned in again.

"How turned on this is making me." She really wanted to turn to see his expression but knew she wasn't supposed to move.

He pulled the machine away again. "Jesus, Becca. You're killing me here."

She grinned. "I asked if you really wanted to know."

An Excerpt from

WILD AT HEART
By T.J. Kline

Bailey Hart has never felt at home in her small
town. So when her band gets their big break
in Los Angeles, "Wild Hart" can't run fast
enough . . . If only there weren't so many reasons
to stay. After a harrowing stint in the Oakland
Police Department, Chase McKee has returned
home a hero, and yet he feels anything but. And
when he finds out Bailey might be leaving for
good, the feelings he's always harbored for his
best friend's cousin just won't stay hidden.

Chase picked up on the roar of the engine long before the motorcycle actually came into view. Reaching for the radar gun, he aimed it in the direction of the sound.

Ninety-two miles per hour. Did this guy have a death wish?

He'd no more tapped the gas on the cruiser when the motorcycle blazed past him in a midnight-blue streak. He flipped on his lights and siren and the bike immediately slowed as the rider glanced backward before pulling onto the shoulder.

At least he has some respect for the law, he thought acerbically as he stopped behind the motorcycle and ran the plates.

The registered owner's name came up on his computer screen and his eyes shot back to the rider.

"Damn it," he muttered, rolling his shoulders back and preparing for the battle he had no doubt was coming. Chase rolled his eyes and climbed out of the vehicle with a sigh of resignation. Crossing his arms, he greeted the most beautiful woman—and the biggest troublemaker—he'd ever met as she slid her helmet off her head and brushed stray hairs back into her low honey-colored ponytail.

"Funny seeing you here, Bailey. When did you get this thing, and are you trying to kill yourself with it?"

She turned her dazzling pearly whites on him, her blue

eyes flashing with mischief as she set the helmet on the seat behind her. Chase had been dying to ask her out ever since his return to town almost two years ago but she had no idea and, unfortunately, he needed to keep it that way. Her cousin Justin was one of his best friends, and if he knew Chase thought of Bailey as anything other than Justin's "little sister," Chase would probably have to arrest his friend for assaulting a police officer. Not to mention that he'd need to check himself into the hospital.

"Just picked it up last week." Her fingers ran lovingly over the blue gas tank between her thighs, and he felt his body immediately react. He stifled the response. "I guess I'm still getting used to how much power it has."

"Ya think?" He couldn't help but chuckle at her understatement as he clicked the top of his pen and started writing out a speeding ticket. "I need your license and registration."

"Aw, come on, Chase. Really?" She bit her lower lip, looking up at him from under her thick, dark lashes, and he felt the heat of desire trickle down his chest and center low in his belly. "I'll slow down. I swear."

"And you'll never do it again, right?" He didn't believe her for a second. Everyone knew Bailey's reputation as the wild child of the Hart family. She didn't just march to the beat of her own drum, she conducted the entire orchestra to a tune of her design.

"You know, you should come by for dinner tonight. I'm fixing enchiladas for them. We're hoping the spicy food will put Jules into labor. There'll be plenty if you want to stop by."

A flirtatious smile spread over her full lips and her eyes sparkled like sapphires. Chase felt the sizzle of heat come to life again. If he didn't know her better, he'd think she was flirting. That was the last thing he needed right now. He turned the pad toward her and handed her the pen, indicating she should sign the line. She stared up at him expectantly, practically batting her eyelashes.

Chase cocked his head to the side and gave her a lopsided grin. "Plying me with dinner isn't going to get you out of a ticket, Bailey."

Her eyes narrowed as he tapped the pad again. Bailey jerked it from his hand and scribbled her name, slapping the pen against it irritably when she finished. He ripped her copy of the citation from the pad and handed it back to her with the other documents. "You *do* realize trying to bribe an officer is a felony, right?"

She cocked a brow at him as she slid her helmet back over her head and slipped her sunglasses on, starting the engine. "Who said anything about bribing you? Maybe I was trying to poison you."

Chase couldn't help but laugh as she eased the bike back onto the road. "Murder One is a felony, too," he yelled after her.

Damn, that woman could turn him on faster than she did that bike.

An Excerpt from

THE BRIDE WORE STARLIGHT
A Seven Brides for Seven Cowboys Novel
By Lizbeth Selvig

Once comfortable on stage in front of thousands, Joely Crockett is now mortified at the thought of walking—or rolling—down the aisle at her sisters' wedding. Scarred and wheelchair-bound, the former beauty queen has lost more than the ability to walk—she's lost her fire. But when one handsome, arrogant guest accuses her of milking her injuries and ignites her ire, Joely finally starts to feel truly alive again, and soon it's impossible for her to resist her heart's desire.

"You look lost."

She started at an unexpected, masculine voice and swung her gaze to the dining room doorway. Her mouth went dry as a summer drought, and her pulse hiccupped before it began to race. The man who stood there with a hot smile and a confident demeanor owned a pair of the sharpest hazel eyes she'd ever seen, sandy-gold hair the color of a palomino stallion, and a jaw and cheekbones strong enough to have been chiseled out of Wyoming granite. Most unsettling of all was a smile that likely could have charmed Sunday school teachers out of their knickers—in any era past or present.

After she'd stared for an impolite number of seconds, Joely lowered her eyes and cupped her chin so her thumb rode up the left side of her in order to hide the scar. She'd convinced herself it made her look thoughtful and masked the self-consciousness she'd never suffered before the accident.

"I might be lost," she said. "But I'm probably not."

"You're Joellen."

"Not unless you're angry at me."

He raised one amused brow. "I'm not."

"Then it's Joely."

"I admit it; I knew that. What I don't know is how a pretty

little thing like you could possibly be sitting all alone like this in a house full of women."

She stared, not sure whether she was annoyed at the "pretty little thing" epithet or surprised at his mind-reading ability, since she'd been wondering the same thing.

"My whole family is in the kitchen through that door. I could ask you the same thing. What's a patronizing cowboy like you doing in my mother's dining room knowing my name when I don't know yours?"

The grin widened, and he strode into the room, dark denim jeans fitted nicely on his hips, a subtle plaid shirt tucked at the waist, and a casual brown sport coat giving him a touch of western class. He reached her in three strides, his cowboy boot heels beating a soft, pleasant cadence on the oak floor. "Alec Morrissey," he said, holding out his hand. "Alexander if you're mad at me."

The name left her stunned again. She knew it. Anyone who followed rodeo knew it. But he couldn't be *the* Alec Morrissey— the one who'd won three PRCA titles and then dropped out of sight half a dozen years ago . . . She shook her head to clear it before she could blurt a question that would sound stupid. She kept her hand over her scar by pretending to scratch her temple and took his hand to shake it. His firm, dry masculine grip sent a small warning shiver through her stomach.

"I'm not," she said.

"Not what?"

"Not mad at you."

"Ah. Even if I'm patronizing? Or if I admit I'm not a real cowboy? Which I'm not, by the way. I wear the boots because they're comfortable."

She wanted to tell him she'd only forgive him if he promised never to call her a pretty little thing again. Her father had called her that, but not in a proud papa kind of way. It had been more a "you're my delicate little flower, don't worry your pretty little head over such things" kind of way. But based on the confidence this man exuded, Joely doubted she could tell him to do or not do anything.

"Well, I can't lie. I'm disappointed about the cowboy part. But if you swear to quit being patronizing, I won't be mad."

He pulled out a chair beside her and sat backward on it, comfortable and easy, looking as if he'd lied about not being a cowboy and straddled seats and saddles every day.

"Ma'am, if calling you pretty is patronizing, I can't swear because any promise I made I would break every time I saw you."